GOLDEN DAYS

(Further Leaves from Mrs. Tim's Journal)

D. E. STEVENSON

LARGE PRINT
Oxford

First published in Great Britain 1934
by
Herbert Jenkins

Published in Large Print 2006 by ISIS Publishing Ltd.,
7 Centremead, Osney Mead, Oxford OX2 0ES
by arrangement with
the Author's Estate

British Library Cataloguing in Publication Data
Stevenson, D. E. (Dorothy Emily), 1892–1973
Golden days. – Large print ed.
1. Highlands (Scotland) – Social life and customs
– Fiction
2. Domestic fiction
3. Large type books
I. Title
813.9'12 [F]

ISBN 0–7531–7612–2 (hb)
ISBN 978–0–7531–7613–9 (pb)

Printed and bound in Great Britain by
T. J. International Ltd., Padstow, Cornwall

FOREWORD

BY THE

VERY REVEREND L. MacLEAN WATT, D.D., LL.D.

Author of *Life and Literature, The Grey Mother, The Tryst*, etc.

This is a book without a murder-mystery or a sex problem in it, yet it is a clear-cut section of real life, with living people and living conversation. You meet them and get to know them just as you meet and get to know friends in daily experience; and their character develops in your continued acquaintance. It leaves you with a feeling that you have been very glad to have met them, and will be glad to meet them again. There is about them an atmosphere that is refreshing and bracing. And when you say goodbye, your hands and hearts are clean. It is an achievement of genius.

CONTENTS

WEDNESDAY: 1ST JUNE

WE TRAVEL NORTH, MEET AN OLD ACQUAINTANCE, AND EVENTUALLY ARRIVE AT OUR DESTINATION

The morning dawns bright and warm, sunshine falls in golden swathes on the faded carpets of Loanhead. The house is filled with the bustle of departure. Gloom descends upon me as I dress, and I follow Tim to the bathroom — where he is shaving — to tell him that I wish I were going south with him.

"Well, you can't get out of it *now*," he replies, scraping fiercely at his chin. "Besides, you need a spot of leave and you're sure to enjoy it when you get there. I only wish *I* had a chance of spending a fortnight in the Highlands. You can think of me grilling in the heat at Biddington and toiling and moiling to get my company into trim — I bet that ass Neil Watt has made a complete hash of it while I've been away."

I am in no whit comforted by the conversation. Of course I have been looking forward to my visit to the Highlands, but the scattering of my family fills me with sadness and a strange fear. Soon we shall be hundreds of miles apart — Tim at Biddington with the Regiment,

Bryan at school, and Betty and I with Mrs. Loudon at Avielochan.

A letter in Mrs. Loudon's firm hand is waiting for me on the breakfast-table — perhaps it is to say she cannot have us after all. This would have been a disaster yesterday, but to-day it would be a reprieve. I scan it eagerly, and find that it is no reprieve, but merely a confirmation of exile. In other words an itinerary of our journey, and a list of various places where we shall have to "change." It also contains the news that Mrs. Loudon's son — a Lieutenant-Commander in His Majesty's Navy — has arrived unexpectedly on leave, and that the house-party is further augmented by a cousin (about whom no information is given). The letter adds to my gloom. I feel convinced that I shall be *de trop* in this family party, and that Mrs. Loudon is now regretting her impulsive invitation to Betty and me. (I am frequently beset with the uncomfortable conviction that people don't really want me and have only asked me from a stern sense of duty. I am told this is really a complex, and probably has its origin in some forgotten episode of my childhood. Complex or no, it seizes upon me at inopportune moments, and makes my life a misery. Often, when bidden to lunch or tea with hospitable friends, it descends upon me suddenly when I am standing upon their doorstep, and wages a battle royal with my common sense, so that I can hardly force myself to ring the bell and enquire if Mrs. So-and-so is at home. This subconscious self of mine insists with devilish plausibility that Mrs. So-and-so did not really want me to come, has now quite forgotten that she asked me, and will be disagreeably surprised when she sees me walk in.)

I point out to Tim (who is now busy stoking up for his journey, with bacon and eggs) that I could send a wire to Mrs. Loudon and tell her I can't come after all.

"Don't be silly, Hester," he says. "You'll enjoy it, and it will do you good. Besides, where would you go? You know how expensive hotels are. We ought to start soon if Bryan is ready."

It is all quite true and sensible. How I wish I were not tortured by vague fears! I retrieve Bryan from the garden, where he has been taking tender farewell of his hedgehog, and pack him into the car.

"There you are!" exclaims Tim, with a cheerfulness which I feel is slightly artificial, "all ready, Bryan? Got the maps?"

Bryan has got the maps safely, and is very proud of having them in his possession. He has also got a compass, and explains to me that this will come in very handy if they should lose their way. As long as they keep due south they can't go wrong, Bryan says. I have a sudden vision of the car rushing due south, over fields and through hedges like a miniature tank, which makes me feel quite hysterical.

There is a slight lull in the activities after their departure, and I become conscious of an empty feeling in my interior — have I or have I not had any breakfast? I decide that I have not, and repair to the dining-room, to remedy the omission, only to find that breakfast has been cleared away. Perhaps I did have breakfast after all, the empty feeling may be due to Tim's departure and not — as I had supposed — to lack of nourishment.

I pay Cook and Maggie and present them with their insurance cards, duly stamped. Maggie says she hopes the new lady will be as nice (this is a typically Scottish compliment and I drink it down with smiles of gratitude, and shake her warmly by the hand). Cook says her hands are wet, and we had better be away if we're thinking of getting the train.

A few minutes later Betty and I, accompanied by the faithful Annie, are on our way to the station in the taxi.

Annie has arrayed herself in a thick black coat with a fur collar, and is obviously prepared for the climatic rigours of the north.

"Your face is very red, Annie," says Betty suddenly. Fortunately Annie is not in the least disturbed by the personal nature of the remark. She replies, amiably, that it's the heat, and I realise afresh that Annie is an ideal custodian for a child.

Our station wears an air of leisure quite unknown to those bustling termini where the trains run southward. The porter greets us with a smile and asks if we are "away for our holidays." He discusses at length the merits of different carriages and, eventually, deposits Betty and me in an empty compartment, with Annie next door.

"You call me if — you know what, ma'am," says Annie mysteriously, as she disappears, and I remember — with a shudder of horror — my last journey with Betty, and send up a silent prayer that Annie's kind ministrations may not be needed.

4

The train is late in starting, having been delayed by the arrival of a large family with mountains of luggage. Nobody minds the delay, there is a happy-go-lucky feeling about the whole affair; the very barrows seem to grumble along in placid way, quite different from the querulous creak of the ordinary station barrow. I can imagine the engine looking round like a fatherly old horse: "You all ready, people?" it enquires kindly. "Quite sure you haven't left anything behind? Well then, off we go."

And off we do go.

Quite soon we are out of the environs of the town; cruising along amongst rolling hills. Whitewashed cottages nestle in green hollows. Cattle standing knee-deep in reeds lift their slow heads and gaze at us with surprise.

Betty eats an orange and discourses in her usual practical manner — scenery has no charms for her.

After about an hour she asks if we are nearly there, and I reply firmly that we shall not be there for hours and hours.

"But we've been hours and hours already," she says, "and we were *in* Scotland when we started so we *must* be nearly there. Scotland's quite small on the map." I decide that it is now time to produce some picture papers, which I have hidden in my bag to beguile the monotony of the journey for Betty and ensure a little peace for myself. Betty seizes upon them eagerly, and forgets all about the dimensions of Scotland in her enjoyment of the antics of Mr. Rhino's scholars.

5

We cross a deep river with a rumble of wheels, and immediately the scenery changes and becomes wild. The rolling hills give place to mountains, which stand back in sullen splendour and allow us to pass. The cattle become sheep, snowy lambs with black wobbly legs and cheeky little black faces interrupt their breakfast to stare at the train. Streams leap down the hillsides amongst the rocks, and dive beneath our wheels to emerge on the other side in beds of gravel and yellow stones. The gorse is like a shower of minted sovereigns, flung down with a careless hand as far as eye can reach.

Now the land falls away, we creep along the shoulder of a hill, and a vista of green valley is disclosed. Farmhouses, with their patchwork of fields, are scattered hither and thither, and on the farther slopes of the mountains, a few wind-swept cottages stand amongst sparse trees.

Suddenly the spell is broken, the door of our compartment is pushed ajar, and through the aperture appears the fat white face of Mrs. MacTurk. Of all the people in the world Mrs. MacTurk is, perhaps, the one I least want to see. I can't help wondering what she is doing in the train, and how she has found me. She must be — I suppose — one of those peculiar people who *walk about* in trains. Why couldn't she have remained peacefully where she was put by the porter amidst her own belongings in (I have no doubt) a comfortable first-class compartment?

"Is this really you?" she says.

I reply that it is. The woman has the knack of saying things which invite a fatuous answer.

"Well I never!" she says.

I fix a false smile upon my countenance, whereupon she insinuates her cumbrous body through the door, and sits down beside Betty.

"So you are going north for a holiday," she says.

Betty bounces up and down on the seat. "Do you know Mummie?" she cries excitedly. "Fancy you knowing Mummie! I thought Mummie didn't know anybody in Kiltwinkle. Of course I knew lots of children at school, but it was awfully dull for Mummie. Mrs. Watt said there would be lots of parties, and Mummie bought a new dress, and then nobody asked her."

I plunge wildly into the conversation, wishing, not for the first time, that Betty were shy with strangers.

"How wonderful the gorse is!" I exclaim rapturously.

It is unfortunate that at this moment we happen to be creeping through a narrow ravine strewn with boulders. Mrs. MacTurk looks out of the window and then at me in surprise.

"This gorge," I scream, above the roar of the train. "So wild and rocky."

"Oh, I thought you said *gorse*," says Mrs. MacTurk.

Her voice is admirably suited for conversation in a railway train, its strident note can be heard with ease. Bridges leap at us with a roar, mountains peer in at the windows and vanish, but above all these earsplitting noises comes the strident voice in futile discourse.

"And where are you bound for?" she asks with a toothy smile.

I am about to reply truthfully to her question when I suddenly remember that Mrs. Loudon "can't abide the woman," and remember also the diplomatic attempts of Mrs. MacTurk to procure an introduction to my prospective hostess. How awkward it will be if Mrs. MacTurk's destination is within motoring distance of Avielochan. It is unlikely, of course, but unlikely things sometimes happen, especially if you don't want them to. On the whole I feel that it will be wiser to conceal the fact of our visit to Mrs. Loudon.

"How is Mr. MacTurk?" I shout.

My red herring is successful, and for some minutes Mrs. MacTurk is to be heard describing the tortures of her husband's rheumatism.

"And Nora," I scream, when Mr. MacTurk's symptoms show signs of waning. "Have you heard from her lately?"

"Poor souls!" says Mrs. MacTurk. "They are away to India in the autumn."

This is no news to me (although I do my best to look surprised) for Nora's husband is in the Regiment, and I was perfectly aware that he was going to India, having been told so by Major Morley (also of ours) not very long ago. The fact that if Neil Watt had not been posted to India, Tim would have had the vacancy is also known to me through the same agency, and precludes me from feeling any grief at the calamity.

"Nora will enjoy India," I bellow.

"That's to be seen," replies Mrs. MacTurk. "It's very unsettling for the poor girl and bound to ruin her complexion. Mr. MacTurk and I were just saying it's a fortunate thing they're not burdened with children, or we should feel obliged to offer them a home at Pinelands. I'm sure I don't know what I should do if I had to move about from one place to another like you soldiers' wives. We've been at Pinelands ten years now — ever since our marriage — and I'm sure I don't know what I would do if we had to leave. There were only three greenhouses when we went, and the garage was most inconvenient for the Rolls, but Mr. MacTurk soon altered all that — and he put in three bathrooms, and built a billiard room — Mr. MacTurk has spent thousands of pounds on the place."

I now ask with well-feigned interest how the Rolls is rolling — and feel annoyed with myself the next moment. "What a hypocrite you are!" says that other Hester who dwells with me in the same skin, and causes me endless trouble. "You know perfectly well you would be delighted to hear the Rolls had come to a bad end. Why do you try to please people, even when you dislike them as you dislike Mrs. MacTurk?" I have no excuse to give for my conduct but am fitly punished for my falseness by having to listen to the detailed history of the Rolls, the Alvis, and the Armstrong-Siddeley, and to the various reasons why none of them is at liberty to convey Mrs. MacTurk to Avielochan, where she is to join her gilded spouse for three weeks' fishing.

9

"Oh, how funny!" cries Betty, jumping up and down in the manner usual to her when moved by excitement. "Are *you* going to stay with Mrs. Loudon *too?*"

Alas for all my efforts! The cat is now out of the bag beyond recall. Mrs. MacTurk's small eyes gleam as she replies that she is going to stay at the Hotel, but it is not far from the house which Mrs. Loudon always occupies, and it will be very nice to see us there.

"You must come and dine with us at the Hotel some evening," she adds hospitably. "When will you come?"

I reply with haste that there is a large house-party at Burnside, and I do not know my hostess's plans, so it would be useless for me to make any engagements.

"Oh well, you can send me a note when you get there and see what's on," says Mrs. MacTurk. "It doesn't matter a bit how many people there are, Mr. MacTurk will be quite glad to see them all — any day will suit Mr. MacTurk and I," she adds blandly.

The worst has now happened, and there is no further need for me to keep up the conversation, nor to try and make my voice audible above the roar of the train. I murmur that I have a headache — which I discover afterwards is absolutely true — and relapse into my corner. Mrs. MacTurk finds me dull and goes away.

We change at various small stations with unpronounceable names, and arrive at Inverquill about tea-time. This is the station for Avielochan, and I am relieved and delighted to see Mrs. Loudon's tall spare figure, clad in its usual shabby fashion, waiting on the platform. For the last hour I have been torturing myself with conjectures as to what I shall do if she is not there.

But there she is, the same strange, shabby, dignified creature who was so kind to me at Kiltwinkle. She is accompanied by a tall dark man, easily recognisable as her son. His resemblance to his mother is striking, and he has the unmistakable brand of *Navy* stamped upon his clean-shaven countenance. Betty takes instantaneous possession of him (she has a habit of appropriating men, which, looking to the future, is somewhat disquieting) and announces to him confidentially, but with great pride, that she was not sick at all. He congratulates her gravely upon her achievement.

"I think it was because the train went along nice and quietly," Betty says. "I like a nice quiet train that stops a lot — don't you?"

"That depends on whether I want to get there quickly or not," replies Mr. Loudon patiently.

Fortunately for me Mrs. MacTurk is too busy marshalling her stupendous array of luggage to be troublesome to anybody except her porter. Our modest suit-cases are disentangled from the pile, and we pack into Mrs. Loudon's roomy Austin for the last stage of our journey.

The road is glaring white in the afternoon sunshine, golden gorse gleams on the hills. Pine woods, carpeted with brown needles and full of dark shadows and golden lights, creep up to the road's edge, and then retreat in soldierly order, leaving the curling white ribbon bare and sunlit as before. The ribbon unwinds over the moor, where a few black-faced sheep with bouncing lambs crop the scanty herbage between

11

patches of brown heather, raising their heads timidly to watch us roll by. The hills divide, showing glimpses of small lochs, delphinium blue in colour, fed with sparkling burns. Far away against the skyline, a ring of purple hills, with small white patches of snow in their crevices, keeps guard over the peaceful land.

The conversation is desultory, and confined to questions regarding our journey. Whether the train was up to time at Dalmawhagger or some name like that, and did we see Ben something or other. Unfortunately none of us is able to answer intelligently. I can't help feeling that Mrs. Loudon is depressed, or has something on her mind — her remarks seem to lack the trenchant note which I remember so well — but perhaps this is merely my imagination, or perhaps the presence of Annie, sitting up very straight on the folding seat in front of us, is embarrassing her.

We are now passing through a small grey-stone village which seems deserted in the bright white sunshine. A few draggled-looking hens scutter out of our way, and a white cur dog snarls at us from an open doorway.

"This is Avielochan," says Mr. Loudon, turning round from his seat beside the chauffeur, and pointing to the houses. "Mother, you are not doing the honours properly. Look at the shop, Mrs. Christie! It is the pride of the countryside — you can buy everything there, except the one thing you happen to want."

We all look at the shop, and Betty, who seems by no means damped by her long journey, says it looks a very small place to have everything, and do they keep pianos?

"I said they had everything except what you want," says Mr. Loudon gravely. "So, of course, if you want a piano they haven't got one, and if you don't want one you don't ask for it."

"It's like Alice in Wonderland," says Betty after a moment's thought. "Jam every other day, but never to-day."

"You've got it exactly," replies Mr. Loudon.

By this time we had left the village far behind; we pass through two gates which have to be opened and shut, run along a pebbly road by the side of a biggish loch, and slow down to take a sharp bend round a huge bush of rhododendrons.

"Here we are! This is Burnside!" cries Mr. Loudon.

The house bursts into view — it is a long, low, whitewashed building with a slate roof which sags a little, as if the hand of Time had pressed it very gently in the middle. It is surrounded on two sides by pines and firs; on the third side a moory hill stretches skywards, and, on the fourth, a green lawn covered with buttercups and daisies leads to an orchard in full bloom. A burn splashes gaily past the door and runs down towards the loch. Clumps of rhododendrons and masses of daffodils are the only flowers; it is a wild garden fitted to its surroundings of mountain and moor. A small path leads to some stepping stones over the burn, the pine woods creep down to a wooden fence; there is a gate in the fence, and the path disappears into the gloom of the woods.

I stand at the door for a few moments drinking in the strange sweetness of the place.

"Is it like you thought it would be?" asks Mrs. Loudon, with her hand on my arm.

"How could I think — this," I reply vaguely.

"You must be starving," she says. "Come away up to your rooms, and we'll have tea whenever you're ready."

The room allotted to me is large and sunny; it has a plain wooden floor, and plain wooden furniture. Somehow it reminds me — though not unpleasantly — of a hospital ward. Betty and Annie are next door.

It is lovely to take off my hat, my headache has quite gone — nobody could have a headache in this sweet piercing air. I note, as I wash my hands, that the water is slightly brown and smells of peat; there is a faint peaty smell about the whole house, mixed with the resinous smell of sun-kissed pines. There are no carpets on the landing or on the stairs, everything has the same bare look as my bedroom — a pleasant change after the crowded, carpeted rooms of Loanhead.

How far away I am from Loanhead in body and spirit! Where are Tim and Bryan? Are they still travelling southward, getting further and further away from me every moment? This is an unpleasant thought, and I decide to drown it in tea.

In the drawing-room I find a bright fire, and a burdened tea-table, and seated near the fire, a small wispy lady of what is usually called an uncertain age, knitting a large shapeless garment in cherry-coloured wool. She looks up at my approach and narrows a pair of short-sighted eyes.

14

"Oh!" she says vaguely. "Elspeth told me about you — you got here all right, did you? I can't remember your name for the moment, but I know it has something to do with music — now who do you think I am?"

She cocks her head on one side and looks at me coyly.

"Dr. Livingstone, I presume?" I reply inanely. I can't think what makes me say it, unless it was the picture of the historic meeting in darkest Africa which caught my eye coming down the stairs. Obviously the greeting is entirely unsuitable to the occasion, and to the lady — no more like the bearded Livingstone than a sheep is like a walrus — I have not even the faint hope that she will understand the allusion, and she doesn't.

"Oh, how funny you should think I was a doctor!" she says, tittering in a lady-like fashion. "That really is *very* funny — I must tell Elspeth about it when she comes down. Of course ladies *are* sometimes doctors nowadays, but I never went in for it. I once had a course of First Aid — that was during the war, of course — but I found the bandaging rather tiring, so I joined a society for providing the soldiers with pocket handkerchiefs instead. It seemed to me such an excellent idea to provide the poor fellows with pocket handkerchiefs. In a battle, for instance," says the good lady, waving her hands vaguely, "so easy to *lose* your pocket handkerchief in a battle, wouldn't it be? We made thousands of them, and sent them to the Front packed in soap boxes — such charming letters we got from the poor fellows."

15

By this time I have pulled myself together, and decided that this must be the cousin, mentioned casually in Mrs. Loudon's letter. I had forgotten the cousin, or, to be more exact, I had imagined the cousin to be of the male sex — a strong silent individual, possibly an Anglo-Indian, and therefore, to be packed off with Mrs. Loudon's son on fishing expeditions, leaving my hostess and myself to chat comfortably together in the garden. (Is there any other woman on earth who would be so foolish as to build up such a detailed picture from a chance allusion to a cousin?)

My airy dreams fall with a crash, and I realise that my visit to Burnside will be absolutely ruined — I feel extremely annoyed with the cousin for being a woman, and with the woman for being here. Why couldn't she have stayed at home for this one short fortnight — or gone to a spa? (She looks like a woman addicted to spas.) I realise, of course, that my feeling is unreasonable, as, being a cousin, she has far more right to be here than I have.

These thoughts pass swiftly through my head, and the lady is still staring at me with unseeing eyes. "Perhaps I should tell you that my name is Mrs. Falconer," she says at last. "I've been hearing about *you*, of course. You live at Kiltwinkle, don't you? I can't say I ever cared very much for Kiltwinkle, but Elspeth *would* settle there. Oh, I remember your name now — *Christie*, isn't it? I knew it had something to do with music — we used often to go and see the Christie Minstrels when we were children; they had black faces and played banjos — *most* amusing. Of course they had nothing to do with *you*, but it is so strange having the same name — such a coincidence."

I am now beginning to feel positively light-headed, but whether this is due to the good lady's volubility, or the effects of the long day in the train with insufficient food I cannot determine.

"I wonder if you are related to some charming people I met at Bournemouth," Mrs. Falconer continues, still with that unseeing stare which seems to have some strange hypnotic power over its victim. "It must have been in 1911 or perhaps 1912 — anyhow, it was a very warm summer and long before the war — they were staying at my hotel — I wish I could remember the name of it. 'Parkfield' or 'Chatterton' or something like that. Such a comfortable hotel it was, with central heating in all the bedrooms. Of course we did not require it, because it was eighty in the shade at the time, but I remember thinking how pleasant it would be in chilly weather."

"Were your friends called Christie?" asks Mr. Loudon, who has come into the drawing-room during Mrs. Falconer's dissertation.

"I think so," she replies. "It was either Christie or Christison, or it might have been Gilchrist — at any rate they were very charming; there was a mother, very aristocratic-looking with white hair, but the story got about that she was on the stage when he married her. Not that I have anything against the stage myself — and, of course, if they were related to Mrs. Christie it couldn't have been true — I'm only telling you what was said in the hotel —"

17

Mrs. Loudon now appears and interrupts the story to enquire about milk and sugar. "Hand Mrs. Christie the hot scones, Guthrie," she says. "Here's a letter from the MacQuills asking us all over to tennis on Monday. Hester, you ought to see Castle Quill while you're here. Millie, take one of these biscuits — I know you like them, and Mary made them specially. She'll be black affronted if none of them are eaten."

We all eat largely of the good things pressed upon us by our hostess, and the conversation paces along very pleasantly, but somehow I can't get rid of the feeling that Mrs. Loudon is not herself; there is something wanting in her manner. I miss those trenchant comments, those dashing pounces which enchanted me at Kiltwinkle.

It is not until we are dressing for dinner that the cause of Mrs. Loudon's depression is made manifest. She calls me into her bedroom in a mysterious manner, and asks me to admire the view. It is indeed admirable, for the trees have been cleared to give a peep of the loch, behind which a thickly wooded hill sweeps upward to meet the sky in a bold curve. To the left the country slopes gently, and is covered with pale green bracken, interspersed by feathery birch trees, their barks like silver in the afternoon sun.

"But you didn't call me in here to admire the view," I point out to her, when I have exhausted my scanty stock of adjectives, and marvelled afresh at the paucity of the English language.

Mrs. Loudon nods. "I've been wearying for you, Hester," she says, taking up a comb from her

18

dressing-table and scraping fiercely at her thick grey hair. "The truth is Guthrie's being chased by a cat, and I've no more idea what to do about it than fly. Millie's no use to talk to — she likes doing the talking herself — and if I can't talk to somebody about it I'll burst. You know the kind of girl, with a cat face — all soft and furry — and red lips from the chemist's shop. Of course, the man has been starved of girls for eighteen months — I'm not blaming him, though how any son of mine can be such a fool — sitting and yearning at her like a codfish."

"I can't imagine him yearning at anyone."

"Wait till you see him," says Mrs. Loudon, threateningly. "I couldn't have imagined it either — Guthrie of all men! Guthrie who's never looked at a girl in his life! I've often wished he'd give me a daughter-in-law — God forgive me for not knowing I was lucky!"

"Where did she meet him?"

"At a dance in Portsmouth — one of the ships gave a dance — and now she's followed him here, and she's staying at the Hotel in Avielochan — 'fishing with Dad,' that's the excuse. 'Fishing with Dad,'" repeats Mrs. Loudon scornfully. "The girl's never fished for anything except men! Oh yes, I'm being nice to her — I hope I know better than to let him see what a scunner I've taken at her — but it's not easy for me to hide my feelings, Hester. Surely at my age a woman should be past the need to wear a false face."

I don't see what help I can be in the matter, and say so as sympathetically as possible.

"Oh well — I was just hoping he'd see the difference," said Mrs. Loudon cryptically. "I was just hoping — perhaps — you would be nice to Guthrie, and that" — here the scheming woman actually has the grace to blush — "and anyway, I'll have someone to talk to."

I can't help laughing at the idea of a staid married woman like myself being cast for the rôle of vamp.

THURSDAY: 2ND JUNE

MORNING IN THE GARDEN — ELSIE
COMES TO TEA — LOVE AND FISHING

Spend the morning lying in a deck-chair in the garden pretending to knit. How glorious to have nothing to do! Mrs. Loudon comes out and consults me about Betty's food. The conversation strays (by some path not retraceable) to Guthrie's infatuation. We are to see the young woman this afternoon, as she has been invited to tea and to fish on the loch afterwards. I realise, after a few moments' conversation, that I am being asked to go out in the boat with them and "prevent anything from happening." The abandonment of her usual direct method of speech shows how much Mrs. Loudon is *bouleversée* by Guthrie's attachment, and I feel so sorry for her that I consent against my better judgment.

Mrs. Falconer strolls down about midday, and remarks that the sun is very hot and the loch very calm. "I can see it from the right-hand corner of my window if I lean out a little," she informs us. "Now where is Guthrie? He should not be wasting his time, you know, Elspeth. Why doesn't he go and fish? He would have no trouble with the boat to-day, the water is as calm as a mill pond, and there is not a suspicion of wind to blow his flies about."

Poor Mrs. Loudon is too upset to battle with Mrs. Falconer; she departs hastily for the house, saying that she forgot to tell Mary about the curds.

"So unrestful," Mrs. Falconer says with a sigh. "Dear Elspeth, we are all so fond of her, but she is *too much* of a Martha. Just to sit here quietly in the golden sunshine, with the pine trees standing on the hill, is not enough. Some people are incapable of admiring the beauties of Nature in silence — don't you agree, Mrs. Christie?" I agree fervently.

Mrs. Falconer continues: "It was in the autumn of 1905 that I first really saw Nature at its best. Before then I was like the man in the poem, who saw a violet by a mossy stone, and it was nothing more. I dare say you may not know the poem, but it is very beautiful, I can assure you. I heard it recited at a concert by a tall man with a glass eye, and it made an indelible impression on my memory. It may have been something to do with the glass eye, which was a slightly different colour from the other one. Very strange, isn't it, how a glass eye remains fixed, while the other one rolls about, but I dare say it would be stranger if they both rolled in different directions."

At this moment a tall form is seen hurrying across the garden. "Guthrie! Guthrie dear!" cries Mrs. Falconer. "Come here and tell us where you have been. You can hold my wool for me — there — like that, dear. No, not over the thumb — move your hands slowly from side to side as I wind. Now we are all comfortable. Did you catch a lot of fish this morning?"

"I didn't try," replies Guthrie, waving his hands in the air like a praying mantis.

"Now Guthrie, that's too bad of you. Fancy wasting a glorious day like this! Tomorrow may be wet for all we know — not so quickly, dear, and keep your hands lower — you know your mother paid pounds and pounds for the fishing, and there you go mouching round as if there were nothing to do."

Guthrie replies, with admirable restraint, that he had to go to the village to fetch meat.

"But if you had caught some nice fish it would have done just as well," says Mrs. Falconer kindly. "However, I dare say you never thought of that, or you would not have gone that long hot walk in the sun. I never was a great one for meat, myself. Dear Papa used to say *that* was the reason I had such a nice complexion. I don't know whether you remember my father, Guthrie; he was a very fine man. His beard was considered one of the finest in the Conservative Club in London."

Guthrie says he never saw Mrs. Falconer's father. I can see that his patience is wearing thin, and welcome the appearance of my daughter. She and Annie have spent the morning down near the loch. Betty approaches, hopping first on one leg and then on the other.

"Oh Mummie," she says breathlessly, "is it dinner yet? The water is frightfully cold, and I've found

23

seventeen tadpoles. Annie is carrying them in my pail. They've got wriggly tails."

The gong rings for lunch.

Guthrie's young woman, who rejoices in the name of Elsie Baker, arrives at tea-time in a Daimler from the Hotel. She is welcomed by Guthrie with servile adoration. Mrs. Loudon smiles grimly, and says she hopes Miss Baker is well; then she turns to the chauffeur and asks him fiercely if he will take his tea in the servants' hall. The poor man is so alarmed by her manner that he says it doesn't matter at all, and he often does without tea, anyway.

"Nonsense," says Mrs. Loudon. "Away with you to the kitchen, and mind and take a good tea while you're about it."

The man disappears hastily, and we all troop into the dining-room.

Miss Baker is attired in a gown of printed *voile* which looks more suitable for a garden-party than for a fishing expedition. She is certainly pretty, and has quite a nice dimple when she smiles. I can see her resemblance to a pussy-cat, something about the short, pointed chin and the way her eyes go up at the corners — green eyes.

Guthrie secures a seat next to his divinity, and admires her, mostly in silence. The rest of us make futile conversation. Mrs. Falconer, from whom I expected a useful flow, seems to have dried up at the source. She reminds me of the rivers of Australia, which, I have been told, are either rushing along in full flood, or else mere stagnant ditches with no refreshment for man nor beast.

Mrs. Loudon, behind two large tea-cosies, whispers to me, "Did you ever see the like?" To which I reply, "Yes, I've seen dozens exactly the same."

Mrs. Falconer pricks up her ears at this, and says, "Dozens of what?" which completely stumps me.

Luckily Mrs. Falconer does not wait long for a reply. She is one of those blessed people who would rather give than receive information. "Aren't people queer?" she says, looking round the table to see if we are all listening. "I once knew a man called Charles Wood, and one day when he was going to Filey by train — or perhaps it was Bristol, I can't be quite certain — he saw a train starting off with Charleswood written on it. And what do you think he did? Well, he jumped into the train and went there, although he had a ticket in his pocket for Filey — or it may have been Bristol — and when he got there, he bought a house and insisted on going there to live, although it was most inconvenient for his work and didn't suit his wife. She was an invalid, of course, having broken her leg out hunting — or it may have been falling off a bus — no, that was somebody else I am thinking of; it was falling off a horse she broke it, but I can't remember, just for the moment, whether that happened before they went to live at Charleswood or after they got there. She disliked the place intensely, it was so awkward ordering things on the telephone — Mrs. Charles Wood, Charleswood — such a muddle it was, for the poor thing."

Guthrie, who has been waiting with ill-concealed impatience for the end of the story, now jumps up and says we had better be getting under way. Whereupon Mrs. Falconer exclaims that these nautical expressions are so intriguing, and how do you spell it? Is it *weigh*? And has it anything to do with weighing the anchor?

"Yes, rather," says Guthrie. "We weigh the anchor every morning to see how much it has lost during the night. You've heard the expression that a ship is losing way, haven't you, Cousin Milly?" And goes out hurriedly, before anything more can be said.

Mrs. Falconer smiles vaguely and repeats her conviction that it is all most intriguing, adding, that if she had a son, she would insist on his going into the Navy just like dear Elspeth. Whereupon "dear Elspeth" replies, uncompromisingly, that she did everything she could to prevent Guthrie from going into the Navy, short of locking him in the toolshed.

We start off for the loch, Guthrie laden with mackintoshes, rollocks, fish-bags, rods, etc. He refuses to let Miss Baker carry anything, but I am allowed to carry the landing-net and a fly-book without any argument. It is still very warm and I am nearly boiled in my tweeds, but have been too well drilled by Tim to think of donning any other garb for a sporting expedition. Miss Baker glides along in her light frock, collecting wild flowers, and looking very charming indeed. Guthrie can't keep his eyes off her, nor reply rationally to my attempts at conversation.

Guthrie sits down in the thwarts, and assembles his rod with the loving care of an experienced fisherman.

His hands look big and clumsy, but they are strangely neat as he threads the reel line from ring to ring. I have made up my mind to assume the rôle of boatman, in which I have had considerable experience when fishing with Tim. So far from any objection being raised at this altruism on my part, I find that both my companions accept it as the obvious solution to the problem. In fact, so far as they are concerned, it is not a problem at all. Feel slightly aggrieved at this, as I should have liked the chance of refusing to throw a cast.

"What are you putting on, Elsie?" says Guthrie, frowning over his flies. His face changes as he looks up and sees her open a large fly-book full of made-up casts.

"These are the ones for Scotch locks," says Elsie brightly.

"I'll show you how to make up your own," he offers with a shy smile.

"But these are the right thing," Elsie replies. "I mean to say they're specially made for Scotch locks; the man in the shop said so."

Nothing more is said about casts, but the next two hours provide an interesting object-lesson in the counter-attractions of love and sport. I feel quite sorry for the wretched girl, she puts her foot in it so often, and so unconsciously. Guthrie starts, like a perfect gentleman, by giving his young woman the best drifts, but begins to tire of the game when she has lost two good trout, dropped her rod into the water, and caught him on the ear with her tail fly.

27

"I'll take the right-hand cast this time," he says as we approach a black rock, which, even to my inexperienced eye, looks a likely spot for a big one.

Suddenly Guthrie's reel screams, and his rod is bent like a hoop: "It's a whopper!" he says excitedly. "Back the boat, Mrs. Christie."

The boat is already backed for Guthrie to play his fish. Twice he brings it up to the boat, and twice it rushes away and lurks beneath the shadow of the rock. Miss Baker has laid down her rod in the boat so as to land Guthrie's fish for him; two of her flies are deeply embedded in my skirt, but the moment is too thrilling for trifles to matter.

"Here we are," Guthrie says, winding in his reel. "The fight's out of him now — well under him, Elsie."

Miss Baker seizes the net, and dashes at the fish excitedly, and the next moment the fish has gone, and Guthrie's line lies limply on the water.

"Good heavens! Have you never landed a fish before?" he cries.

"Of course I have," replies Elsie hotly. "I always land them for Dad — that one wasn't hooked properly —"

"Hooked? Of course it was hooked — you knocked the hook right out of its mouth."

Elsie looks at him with dewy eyes.

"Never mind," he says hastily. "I expect it was my fault — better luck next time."

Peace is restored. We try another drift — a good one near some weeds. This time Miss Baker catches herself.

I am about to back away from the weeds to rescue the damsel in distress when Guthrie says: "Never mind just now, Mrs. Christie, we'll just *drift gently on to the weeds* — keep the boat round a little for me. That's great!"

There is a light in his eye that I have seen before in Tim's — I know the meaning of it well. I edge the boat gently along, hardly daring to breathe. Meanwhile, Miss Baker struggles wildly to disentangle the Greenwell's Glory from the lace of her hat — I can see she is anxious not to tear the lace.

Suddenly a trout rises and turns over Guthrie's tail fly, eyeing it with suspicion. He casts again over the same place, and the next moment his reel is running out.

"You've got him!" I cry breathlessly.

We back out of the drift, and I land a beautiful fat trout for him with great success.

"I've torn the lace," says Elsie, with a singular lack of discernment. She ought — of course — to have admired Guthrie's trout.

"I say, what a pity!" Guthrie says sympathetically. "And it's such a pretty hat, too — must be a pound-and-a-half at least," he adds, gazing with admiring eyes at the still wriggling trout with its spotted sides and silver scales. Elsie replies that it was three guineas, but Guthrie is not listening; he is planning a fresh campaign.

"We might try the bay on the north side," he says. "I've often got a good fish over there."

· It has suddenly become colder, and a nice breeze has got up. The bitter-sweet smell of sun-warmed gorse comes in an occasional hot whiff of scent over the

29

cooling water. Miss Baker shivers, and remarks that she thinks we had better go in now.

"Good Lord!" cries Guthrie. "We've only just started. *You* don't want to go in, do you, Mrs. Christie?"

"Oh, no! This is the best time of day," I reply. I feel rather a traitor to my sex, but comfort myself by the reflection that it is for Mrs. Loudon's sake. I hope the girl will not get pneumonia or I shall feel like a murderer. Miss Baker evidently realises that she has not shown to advantage as a fisherwoman; she offers to take the oars for a bit, so we change places and try the north bay. Guthrie is torn between his fondness for the new boatwoman and annoyance at her inefficiency.

"That's right, Elsie!" he says. "You're doing splendidly — keep her out a bit more, can't you see you're drifting over the best bit of water? You're an excellent boatman. Good Lord, don't splash like that, you're frightening every fish in the loch! Keep out, keep out — splendid — we're sure to get one in a minute — don't let the boat turn round like that —"

By this time the wretched girl is blue with cold. Even Guthrie sees it. He looks at her appraisingly, and says she ought to have *put more on*. "Perhaps we had better land you," he adds kindly. Miss Baker jumps at the suggestion, and we row back to the boat-house.

"You'll come, too, won't you, Guthrie?" she says, as she watches him land her rod and fishing-tackle.

Guthrie hesitates; he looks at the loch, which is covered with small ripples from shore to shore. "Well," he says, "I think, if you don't mind, we'll go on for a bit

— we've only got one so far — and you can easily find the way up to the house — it's no distance — just follow the path, you can't go wrong."

Miss Baker looks surprised and disappointed, but has the sense not to make a scene. Their "good-bye" can be no more than friendly, with me sitting in the boat. Guthrie does not think of leading her behind the boat-house, his mind is too full of ripples; he does not even follow her with his eyes as she trips gracefully up the path, carrying her rod and fly-book.

We fish until nine o'clock, and return tired and cold, but at peace with the world. Our bag consists of nine good trout, of which two are mine.

FRIDAY: 3RD JUNE

A LAZY MORNING —
MRS. FALCONER TALKS

Mrs. Loudon having disappeared into the kitchen, I find my way to the flower-room with the laudable intention of helping my hostess by doing the flowers for her (I rather pride myself on my skill in this branch of domestic economy). I am discovered in the act by Mrs. Loudon, who has polished off her house-keeping in record time.

"You'll take your hands off those flowers at once," she says fiercely. "What do you think you're here for? You're here for a holiday, my girl, and don't you let me catch you doing a hand's turn in this house or I'll pack you into the next south train, bag and baggage."

Fortunately I am sufficiently acquainted with my hostess not to be alarmed by her ferocity, so I merely put my arm round her waist, and give her a little squeeze.

"You and your blandishments!" she says scornfully, but is quite pleased all the same.

Mrs. Loudon's idea of doing the flowers is to cram every receptacle as full as she possibly can. I remain and offer a few words of advice on the subject, although

I am not allowed to touch them. Suddenly she throws the flowers into the sink, and seizing me by the arm, demands in a hoarse whisper, "Hester, how did you do it? I've been wondering the whole night long. How on earth did you get rid of her?"

I reply that I made a cold breeze spring up, and covered the loch with the most fascinating ripples.

"Well, I wouldn't put it past you," she says, with a twinkle in her eye. "I may tell you the lassie was starved with cold when she got here — frozen to the marrow. I couldn't help feeling a bit sorry for her."

I reply that I was sorry for her, too, and that I trust she will not die of pneumonia.

"Not she. I gave her a good dose of cherry brandy" — this is Mrs. Loudon's panacea for every ill, and not a bad one either. "And now away with you," she adds in her normal voice. "I'll never get these flowers dressed with you standing there trying to cram your new-fangled notions down my throat" — here she forces three more wretched tulips into an already bursting vase. "Away with you into the garden. Take a book with you, and give an old woman some peace."

So I depart into the garden with a book; but I have no intention of reading it. Instead, I lie in a long chair, and look at the mountains. Small clouds are trailing grey shadows over their calm bosoms. There is a single pine tree on the lower slopes, so near, it looks, that I could almost reach upward and pick it. The things pertaining to Martha fall away from me, and a blessed feeling of idleness encompasses my soul. I have not got to remember anything — neither to order fish, nor to count the washing. I need not write an order for the grocer, nor hunt after Maggie to see if she has cleaned the silver and brushed the stairs. The condition of Cook's temper is of no consequence to me, there are no domestic jars to be smoothed over. No sudden appeals to my authority, requiring the wisdom of Solomon and the diplomacy of Richelieu, can disturb my peace.

My thoughts drift across the garden and hang upon the trees like fairy lights, or curl upwards and vanish like the smoke of Burnside chimney. I can take a thought from the cupboard of my memory — just as I take a dress from my wardrobe — give it a little shake and put it on, or fold it away.

A bird singing in a pear tree brings back my childhood, and an orchard knee-deep in grass. Richard stands before me with the sun shining in his fair hair. "Have a bite, Hessy," he says — and the strange sour tang of that pear makes my mouth water at this very moment.

How nice it is to lie here in blameless idleness, and let these vagrant memories flow through my body like a cool stream!

Somewhere in the world there must be a formula (am I trembling upon the edge of it now?) which, could I but grasp it, would reveal to me the Secret of the Universe. For there must be a secret, of course; the world would never roll over and over on its way through Time and Space if everyone's thoughts were as vagrant and purposeless as mine. This secret, once known, would string my thoughts together like a necklace of pearls.

But where to look for the secret — where to find it? Those mountains, dreaming so peacefully in the sunshine — do they possess it? Could I wrest it from their eternal silence? Shall I find it in the swallow's jagged flight, as it darts across the garden in pursuit of flies? Shall I find it in the call of the cuckoo, echoing sadly from the pine-clad hills? Or is it hidden deep in the hearts of human beings — a piece here and a piece there — so that if you could find all the pieces and fit them together, the puzzle would be complete? But the hearts of human beings are so difficult to find — people are so sealed up in themselves, withdrawn behind impenetrable barriers.

A bee drones past seeking honey in the golden bells of the daffodils — from one to another he quests with intermittent buzz. Are the flowers secret to him as people are to me? Or does he, tasting their sweetness, taste the very essence of their being, and know their souls? . . .

"Oh, to be in England now that May has come!" exclaims a rapturous voice from behind my chair. (I have been so deep in thought that I have not heard Mrs. Falconer's approach.) "Only, of course, we are in Scotland really — and it's June. Perhaps you don't know the poem I was quoting, Mrs. Christie. It is by a man called Byron — or was it Rupert Brooke? No," she continues, sitting down beside me and producing her knitting. "No, it couldn't have been Rupert Brooke, because he only wrote things about the war (although he did write something about 'England being here,' I know), but I remember learning *this* poem in 1892 when I was quite a child. I really was *quite* young at the time, but I have never forgotten it. Us girls did not go to school. Papa did not approve of school for girls. We were taught at home by a Miss Posten — such a very ladylike woman, she was, and most accomplished."

I murmur feebly that I feel sure she must have been.

"Yes, indeed, *most* accomplished," says Mrs. Falconer complacently. "I always think us girls owe a lot to Miss Posten, and I make a point of saying so whenever possible. I think it is only right to give people their due. I never saw anybody who could make a ribbon-work rose so beautifully as Miss Posten. It was so like a real rose that I used to tell her the birds would come and peck at it if she left it out of doors. Just like that artist who painted a picture of fruit, and the birds pecked at it because they thought it was real. I can't remember the name of the man, but Miss Posten always enjoyed the little joke."

Mrs. Falconer flows on until the gong sounds for lunch. We take our usual places round the table, and I proceed to enjoy the excellent food, which tastes all the better because I have not ordered it.

"Well, Guthrie, dear!" says Mrs. Falconer as she unfolds her table-napkin, "I haven't seen a hair of you all the morning. You remember, Elspeth, what a favourite expression that was with dear Papa — I have not seen a hair of you, he used to say."

Mrs. Loudon replies, rather shortly, that she has no recollection of hearing Mrs. Falconer's father make use of the expression.

"Oh, but you *must* remember, Elspeth. Hardly a day passed but he would come out with it. How we used to laugh! — 'I haven't seen a hair of you all day' — Papa had the *drollest* way of saying things. And have you seen Miss Baker, Guthrie? Aha, you naughty boy! — I'm sure that's where *you've* been."

Guthrie admits sulkily that he met Miss Baker in the village.

Mrs. Falconer laughs. "I can't help laughing," she says. "Such a funny name — BAKER — isn't it? I always expect to see her hands all covered with flour, don't you?"

Guthrie replies with asperity: "No more than I expect to see you with a hawk on your wrist."

"A hawk!" cries Mrs. Falconer. "My dear Guthrie, you need never expect to find *me* having anything to do with a *hawk*. Horrible creatures, pouncing down out of the sky and picking out your eyeballs. I once read a book about India which said that there was a hawk waiting in the sky every three miles. It made me feel quite creepy, and took away all my desire to go to India. Snakes I *could* bear, but hawks every three miles — no, no!"

"Those were kites," Guthrie says, handing in his plate for a second helping of meringue. (I notice that, like most men, he has a very sweet tooth.)

"Kites? Oh no, Guthrie dear! It was I who read the book, and you must really allow me to know best. A kite isn't a bird at all; it is a sort of box made of paper. One of the boys had one the year we went to Littlehampton (you remember me telling you about the year we went to Littlehampton, Elspeth?). He sailed it on a long piece of string. It always puzzled *me* how it stayed up in the air. Well, one day there was a high wind, and Edward's kite went sailing over the housetops. We had a great hunt for it, and eventually we found it hanging on a rope in somebody's garden, all amongst the clean clothes, and the clothes were so beautifully white that Mama decided, then and there, to send our linen to the woman to wash. The laundry we had before used to send the things home a sort of grey colour, and we found afterwards that they were hung out to dry next to the station yard. Well, that was all very well, and the linen was beautifully done, but things went amissing — first one of Papa's collars, and then a very beautiful embroidered tablecloth which my grandmother had brought home from India. It was embroidered with elephants with hurdles on their backs — so quaint! There was an ivory fan as well, all made out of elephant's tusks, but Mama broke it when she was out at dinner one night. Dear me, what *was* the name of those people? I'm sure it began with a W. Elspeth, you must surely remember the people I mean. Papa and Mama used often to dine with them, they lived in Holland Park, and kept a pug. I believe it was Abernethy or Golding, or something like that. Anyway, he was a Jew and very rich. So strange, isn't it, that Jews never eat pork. I'm very fond of roast pork myself, but I must say I find it very indigestible."

"Shall we have coffee on the veranda?" says Mrs. Loudon suddenly.

38

SATURDAY: 4TH JUNE

GUTHRIE AND I VISIT THE LAUNDRY

"Up the airy mountain
Down the rushy glen
We daren't go a-hunting
For fear of Little Men."

Guthrie Loudon and I are on our way to the laundry to make enquiries about a garment belonging to Mrs. Falconer, which has failed to return from the wash. Guthrie is acting as guide (for the washer-lady lives in a remote spot, and pursues her useful calling in the wilds). I am to be spokesman, since the missing garment cannot be enquired for by the opposite sex.

I am aware that the garment in question is hand-made, in pink *crêpe de chine*, trimmed with Valenciennes lace — these salient facts having been communicated to me in mysterious whispers by the owner. Mrs. Falconer has spent the morning bewailing her loss, so that our expedition has been undertaken for the sake of peace. I can't make myself believe that it really matters very much whether the expedition is successful or not; the Highland air has this strange effect upon me, that I care for nothing but the enjoyment of the moment — and the moment is exceedingly enjoyable.

Guthrie takes up the song where I left off.

> "Wee Folk, good Folk
> Trooping all together,
> Green jacket, red cap,
> And white owl's feather."

He has a nice deep bass voice, which rolls up the narrow path between the trees, and echoes amongst the rocks.

"It's a good thing we're not superstitious," he says, when the last echo has died away. "The Little People don't like being spoken of, you know. Wouldn't you be frightened if they came crowding down on us out of their hiding-places in the glen, and led us astray?"

"What would they do to us, I wonder."

"They would bind us with silken cords, and keep us prisoners for a hundred years," he replies with relish.

"Then in a hundred years, you and I would return to the world," I tell him. "I wonder whether we should be old and white-haired, or eternally young, like Mary Rose."

"We shall be young," Guthrie decides, "and we shall make lots of money by going about giving lectures, and telling people what a strange place the world was a hundred years ago."

This is the right sort of nonsense for a Highland afternoon, and we elaborate the theme with a wealth of fantastic detail.

"We'll start by telling them about meals," Guthrie continues. "People will be horrified and disgusted when

40

we tell them that we used to sit down round a table four times every day and feed in company. A hundred years hence nobody will dream of eating in public. Each person will retire to his room once a day and swallow enough tablets of protein and carbo-hydrates to last him for twenty-four hours."

"It sounds a little dull," I protest.

"That may be, but eating in public is a relic of barbarism, and it is better to be dull than disgusting. A pretty woman looks her worst at meal-times, and a greedy man is the foulest sight on earth. I knew a fellow who applied to be transferred to another ship, simply because he couldn't stand the sight of the owner eating soup."

While we are thus talking the path curves upward, and there are hundreds of little flowers in the grass — blue and yellow and white and mauve. A few gay butterflies flutter across from side to side, and the sunshine falls like golden largesse between the shadows of the leaves. We emerge from the woods on to the shoulder of a hill — and pause for a moment to admire the view. The air is so clear that the pine trees seem conscious of the lochs, and the lochs seem conscious of the pine trees, as if they were whispering to each other some secret message of their own. A scroll of smoke, from a small farmhouse, hangs in the still air like a smudge of dirt on the blue gauze of the sky. Everything is crystal clear, bright, bright like spring water, like diamonds, like the wide tear-washed eyes of a young child. Brightness seems to me the most astonishing quality of this new world. The brightness of it washes through my body and brain, until I feel clear all through, until I feel utterly transparent, and the sweet hill wind blows through my very soul — cool, lovely clean wind. Every branch of every tree has a song of its own, and the note of the cuckoo echoes from the hills.

"What would you say if I told you we were lost?" says Guthrie suddenly, in a conversational tone. I reply instantly that I should be extremely angry, and cancel his pilot's certificate.

"Well, I told you the Little People would be angry," he says deprecatingly.

We sit down upon the brown carpet beneath an enormous fir-tree and light cigarettes. "You see," he explains, "I thought we might take a short cut. The woods are lovely, aren't they? Are you enjoying yourself?"

"That's neither here nor there," I reply sternly. "We were sent out upon a definite mission — to recover Mrs. Falconer's — er — property at all costs. I am surprised and pained to find that a naval officer, of your service, has so little sense of responsibility."

"Oh damn!" exclaims Guthrie, without rancour. "What does it matter about Cousin Millie's pants, as long as you are enjoying yourself? Can't you see how much more important the one thing is than the other? Try to cultivate a sense of proportion — Hester."

"Certainly, Guthrie," I reply meekly.

He rolls over and looks at me. "You don't mind, do you?"

"Why should I? Everyone calls everyone else by their Christian names nowadays."

"Oh, but this is different!" he says, wrinkling his forehead with the effort to explain. "You're not like everyone, or I would have done it without thinking — and I've been trying to do it all the afternoon — so you see it's different, and I'm doing it differently."

"Well, in that case perhaps I had better say 'no,'" I reply primly.

He looks at me quickly, to see if I really mean it.

"Guthrie, do you smell a lovely smell of peat smoke?" I ask, trying to look very innocent.

"Hester, I believe I do," he replies gravely.

We walk on about fifty yards through a little wood, and come upon a clearing amongst the trees. The sunshine fills it with a golden haze — it is like a bowl of gold. In the middle is a thatched cottage, and all about are lines of rope, with dozens of cheerful garments hung upon them to dry.

"Why, here we are after all!" exclaims Guthrie, and, as I follow him down the path, bending my head beneath a snowy sheet, and dodging the dancing legs of some pale pink pyjamas — are they Guthrie's, I wonder — I can't help suspecting that we were never lost at all.

Miss Campbell receives us with a natural dignity. She is a woman of about forty, tall and straight, with blue-black hair drawn into a knot at the back of her shapely head. "Come away in and have a drink of milk," she says hospitably, as she squeezes the soap-suds off her hands, and wipes them on her checked apron. "Did you walk all the way from Burnside, then?"

"We did," replies Guthrie. "It was a lovely walk. I don't know when I've enjoyed a walk so much. Mrs. Christie has a message for you."

"Is that so?" says Miss Campbell. "I hope it's not to complain of anything, then."

I disclose my errand while Guthrie, with great delicacy of feeling, interests himself in the pictures which adorn the walls. A highly coloured oleograph of a young man offering his heart to a beautiful lady in a Grecian garden seems to claim his particular attention. I can't help wondering whether he sees any resemblance to Elsie in the classic profile of the lady, or is taking hints from the picture as to the exact position it would be correct to assume when he pops the question himself.

"If Mrs. Christie would just come into the laundry a minute," suggests Miss Campbell, in mysterious whispers.

We repair at once to the laundry, a long wooden shed, redolent with the warm smell of freshly ironed clothes. A young girl — tall and dark like Miss Campbell, and with the same graceful and dignified manner — is busily engaged in ironing a pile of fine garments.

"Morag, would you be after seeing Mrs. Falconer's cami-knickers?" asks Miss Campbell bluntly.

"I would not," replies the girl, raising her head and looking at us with a pair of night-blue eyes.

"Where would they be, then?"

"You might be after finding them upon the lines," suggests Morag, after a moment's thought.

44

I follow Miss Campbell into the garden. "I suppose that is your niece," I remark conversationally. "She is very like you."

"She might be," is the cryptic reply, but whether this refers to the likeness or the relationship remains in doubt.

The lines run in all directions like a gigantic spider's web. Miss Campbell looks about her with some pride. "It's a pleasure to be washing some people's clothes," she says, "and to wash for some people is no pleasure at all. You would be surprised, Mrs. Christie, if you could be seeing the things some people wear. It's whited sepulchres, they remind me of, and others, that you might not give the credit to, are all glorious within. It gives you a sight into human nature to wash. See what a pretty line this is! These things belong to Miss MacArbin, now. They are fine and pretty, but quite plain. I like things to be plain, for they come up so nice in the ironing."

I agree with Miss Campbell, and admire Miss MacArbin's taste.

"Miss MacArbin has a lot of new things lately," she continues. "I'm wondering if she will be thinking of marrying. Would you be hearing anything of that nature about Miss MacArbin?"

I reply that I have not the pleasure of her acquaintance.

"That's a pity now. I think you would like Miss MacArbin — she is a very pretty young lady, and clever with her hands. She makes all her own clothes, for they are not well off now, though they own a great deal of property. I would not be surprised to be hearing of her marriage. It's a pity you do not know her. There will be a baby coming to The Hall," continues Miss Campbell, passing down another line full of tiny garments, white as snow. "I like to wash baby-clothes best of all."

I perceive that Miss Campbell — like most people who are buried in the wilds — takes a keen interest in the affairs of her neighbours, and this is her strange manner of keeping a hand on the pulse of life. It must be an amusing game, on long winter evenings, to guess at the meaning of a christening robe amongst the washing from Mrs. A, and to deduce the possibility of an early marriage for Miss B from the fact that she has invested in half a dozen *crêpe de chine* nightdresses.

"Of course I was aware that Mr. Guthrie was home from sea," continues Miss Campbell, confidentially, as she runs her eyes down a line hung with gentleman's underwear, and moves on. "But I could not be placing *you* at all. You are not so plain as Mrs. Loudon herself, nor yet so frilly as Mrs. Falconer. I was wondering could you be Mr. Guthrie's betrothed — but then there was the little girl to account for. Is it your little girl that has the wee pyjamas with the pink collars, then?"

We have been all round the garden by this time without any success. Miss Campbell says we'll take one more look down Miss MacArbin's line —

"Ah!" she says suddenly. "This will be the thing we are looking for. The idea of Morag putting it on Miss MacArbin's line — foolish lassie — it is not like Miss MacArbin at all, at all. Miss MacArbin has a different style altogether."

We retrieve Mrs. Falconer's despised garment from the line, and Morag irons it, and makes it up into a neat parcel.

Guthrie has made an exhaustive survey of the pictures in Miss Campbell's sitting-room, and is now pawing the ground like a restive horse. "You might have *made* the things, the time you took," he says crossly. "You don't mean to tell me they're in *that* parcel! There can't be much *warmth* in them."

He stuffs the parcel into his pocket, and, after taking a polite farewell of Miss Campbell, we set off home.

SUNDAY: 5TH JUNE

I ACCOMPANY MY HOSTESS TO CHURCH

I accompany my hostess to the parish church. We take our seats near the back, and Mrs. Loudon points out some of the notabilities of the neighbourhood as they arrive. Chief among these are Sir Peter and Lady MacQuill, to whose ancestral halls we have been bidden. Sir Peter is a square man with reddish hair and a pink face, his kilt swings in an authoritative manner as he strides up the aisle in the wake of his lady to the front pew.

"She was a MacMarrow of Auchwallachan," says Mrs. Loudon in an awed whisper, and I conclude that this must be a great distinction. I feel glad that Mrs. Loudon has told me about Lady MacQuill, for she looks as if she might easily have descended from that well-known family the Smiths of Peckham. It is her spouse who carries all the dignity of the MacQuills, and his broad shoulders look capable of bearing it.

We speak to them afterwards at the church gate, and they profess themselves charmed to have my company at the tennis-party tomorrow.

"Guthrie asked Hector if he could bring a friend of his, who is staying at the hotel," adds Lady MacQuill, "a Miss Baker, I think it was. Please tell him we shall be delighted to see her."

Mrs. Loudon tries to look pleased at this information, but makes a poor job of it.

"I hope you are making a long stay this year, Mrs. Loudon," says Sir Peter, somewhat in the manner of a king inviting a foreign duchess to settle in his kingdom.

"I'm staying six weeks," replies Mrs. Loudon bluntly.

"Are you enjoying your visit here, Mrs. Christie?" he enquires.

"It is an enchanting spot," I reply gravely.

After this exchange of courtesies, the MacQuills step into the car — an exceedingly ancient and battered Rolls — and are whirled away.

"They're pleasant folk when you get to know them," says Mrs. Loudon, as we return home. "If *he* could forget for a moment that he was Sir Peter MacQuill he'd be easier to speak to — there's no nonsense about *her*. You'll enjoy seeing Castle Quill. Parts of it date from the twelfth century."

Later in the day I find myself strolling with my hostess in the walled garden. This lies upon the hillside some distance from the house. It is a delightful spot with a southern aspect, where vegetables and flowers riot together in happy confusion. I remark on the strangeness of the proximity of onions and sweet-peas, and point out a single damask rose amongst the potatoes.

"That's Donald," says Mrs. Loudon. "It's a little puzzling till you get used to it. But I could never complain to the MacRaes about Donald. The man's a poet, and you have always to make allowances for poets in practical matters. Why, there's the man himself pottering about in his Sunday suit! He can't keep away from his flowers — sometimes I think they're more to him than his children. Donald, here's Mrs. Christie wanting to know why you've got your sweet-peas planted amongst the onions."

The man rises slowly from his knees, and takes off his hat with a natural grace. He is very tall and broad-shouldered, and his rugged face is full of the grandeur of his native hills. These people seem to have more bone in their faces than their southern neighbours — I can't describe it better than by comparing them to their mountains, whose rocks show boldly through the thin covering of earth. A slow smile spreads over Donald's face at Mrs. Loudon's words, and he replies in a soft low voice, "Perhaps I wass thinking it would be pleasant to be smelling the sweet-peas when I would be picking up the onions for Mrs. Loudon's dinner."

"There," says Mrs. Loudon triumphantly. "I knew Donald would have some poetical reason for it."

We move on slowly in the warm air, and Mrs. Loudon begins to talk about Mrs. Falconer. "Sometimes I get deaved with the woman," she admits, "and then I'm sorry. There was a tragedy in her life. You'll have noticed that in all her havering she never mentions her husband. Harry Falconer was a gem. Some of us never understood what he saw in Millie, but that's neither here nor there. They were married, and away they went to Paris for their honeymoon. Three weeks of it they had, and then, one day, they ran after a tram — they were going out to Versailles, or some such place. I don't know the rights of it, for the poor soul never mentions a word about it, but, apparently, Harry suddenly collapsed — the man must have had a weak heart, and nobody knew, not even himself. He died before they could get him back to the hotel. So that was the end of Millie's happiness, poor soul, and that's why I have her here when I can, and bear with her as patiently as I am able — which isn't very patiently, I'm afraid, when all's said and done, because I'm an impatient old woman by nature. Millie was always a talker," continues Mrs. Loudon, after a little pause. "But it wasn't until after she lost Harry that she became so — so trying to her friends. I sometimes think the shock must have affected her brain. They say we're all a wee thing mad on some subject or other."

"Well, what are *we* mad about?" I ask, giving her arm a little squeeze.

"I'm mad about yon girl of Guthrie's," says Mrs. Loudon in a strained voice. "I declare I can think of nothing else, and, if I do think of other things, the girl is nagging away at the back of my mind, for all the world like an aching tooth. Sometimes I think if I could just get him out of her clutches I'd die happy."

"He's not married yet," I pointed out optimistically.

"No, but he's on his way to it," she replies. "You don't think I'm wrong to try to influence Guthrie's life, do you, Hester?"

"She's not the right person for him."

51

"She's all wrong in every way. I'm not that despicable creature, a jealous mother. I'd welcome any girl I thought would make the man a good wife. Someone like you," she continues, looking at me, almost with surprise. "Yes, somebody exactly like you. And I'd steal you from that Tim of yours if I could, but I know there's little hope of that — that's the sort of woman I am. People must marry, and have children — and yet I don't know why I should think so, for there's a deal of sorrow comes to most married folks that single ones escape."

"There are two to bear it," I tell her.

"Yes," she says. "That's the secret, and perhaps sad things don't happen to everybody."

"If we don't have troubles sent us we can generally make them for ourselves," I reply. "It's easy to make yourself miserable over trifles; I've done that sometimes, and then, quite suddenly, you get sent something to be sorry about, and you think — looking back — how happy I was yesterday, and I never knew it."

"Well, well!" she says. "It's all true, but these are sad croakings for a June day. I'll tell you what *you're* mad about now, just to show there's no ill-feeling. You're mad about that good-for-nothing husband of yours. You needn't waste your breath denying it, for I could see it in your face when there was all that talk of his going off to India without you. Oh yes! You're doing without him fine at the moment, but I'm not sure that your heart's really here. Part of you is away south, at Biddington, and you're wishing every now and then that Tim were here."

I am somewhat surprised that Mrs. Loudon should have guessed the state of my feelings so shrewdly, for I have not owned — even to myself — that I am missing Tim. "Perhaps I am missing him," I reply thoughtfully. "But it is really only because it is so lovely here."

"'Never the time, and the place, and the loved one all together,'" says Mrs. Loudon. "But what about suggesting to the man when you write him — if you ever do find time to write him, of course — that he might come up for a few days at the end of your visit, and take you away south with him?"

This sounds a delightful plan, and I say so with suitable expressions of gratitude — at the same time pointing out that Tim may not be able to get leave, and that the journey is expensive.

"Hoots!" she says, twinkling at me in her comical manner. "The man will get leave if he asks for it. I never knew a soldier that couldn't. And as for the journey, he has only to cook up a railway pass — or whatever they call it — and he'll get here and back for nothing."

Mrs. Loudon's ideas of the Army seem slightly out of date. I point out to her that the Golden Age has passed away, but she pays no heed to my expostulations.

"Tell him to come, and he'll come," she says.

By this time we have reached the house. Betty's face appears at the bathroom window. "Come and see me in my bath, Mrs. Loudon," she calls out. "Come *now*. I'm all bare and ready."

Mrs. Loudon waves her hand. "I'll come and skelp you, then," she cries, and away she goes, running like a girl.

MONDAY: 6TH JUNE

THE GARDEN PARTY AT CASTLE QUILL

Castle Quill is approached by a drawbridge over a narrow ravine, at the bottom of which a swift river runs amidst rocks and ferns. The castle is of grey stone, with small dark windows which frown threateningly at the approaching guest.

We drive up to a nail-studded door, and are presently ushered through a large hall, paved with stone and hung with antlers, into an old-fashioned drawing-room, full of furniture of the uncomfortable Early Victorian time. The Castle is a strange blend of periods; it is lighted with electric light, and warmed by central heating, yet these concessions to modern comfort seem to fit into the ancient place, and the whole conglomeration of the ages is blended into an harmonious whole. Perhaps this is due to the atmosphere of the MacQuills, which fills the place. They have lived here ever since the Castle was built, and the very stones are impregnated with their spirit.

The windows of the Victorian drawing-room open on to fine lawns, flanked by herbaceous borders. Here the garden party is in full swing. We are greeted by the laird and his lady with hospitable warmth.

"Hector is somewhere about," says Lady MacQuill vaguely. "He is managing the tennis, I think."

Mrs. Loudon says we will find him, and we walk slowly towards the courts, stopping on the way to speak to various friends of Mrs. Loudon's, to all of whom I am introduced with pleasant old-world formality. Guthrie has now disappeared — probably to look for Miss Baker — so we find two chairs, and sit down to watch the people, and enjoy their peculiarities.

Mrs. Loudon points out "the Duchess," a small fat woman who — at first glance — might easily be mistaken for somebody's cook, but on closer examination is seen to be endued with a strange mantle of dignity befitting her rank.

"Who's that man?" says Mrs. Loudon suddenly. "He seems to know you, Hester, or is he trying to give you the glad eye?"

I look up and am amazed to see Major Morley — of all people — making his way towards us over the grass.

"It's Major Morley!" I gasp.

"What?" says Mrs. Loudon. "Not the man who came to see you at Kiltwinkle? Fancy him following you here!"

I reply hastily that he can't have "followed me here," for the simple reason that he did not know I was coming, and that he only came to see me at Kiltwinkle to relieve my mind about Tim being posted to India. (It was entirely due to Major Morley's machinations at the War Office that Tim got the Home Battalion, and I feel suitably grateful to him for using his influence on our behalf.)

Mrs. Loudon says, "The man's evidently an altruist."

By this time he has reached our retreat. "I've been looking everywhere for you," he says warmly.

"But how did you know I was here?" I enquire.

"Hector MacQuill told me. I'm staying at the Hotel, you know. It's quite a comfortable place, and the fishing's fairly good."

It is very nice to find a friend amongst all these strangers, and Major Morley is usually amusing. He and Mrs. Loudon take an instant liking for each other — an occurrence which pleases and surprises me in equal proportions. They are both outspoken and definite in their ideas, and they both possess a dry sense of humour. I feel they might just as easily have hated each other at first sight — and this would not have been nearly so pleasant.

We sit and talk about our fellow guests — Major Morley seems to be acquainted with many of their foibles. The conversation is not easy to follow for one who does not know the district.

"Have you seen the MacDollachur girl?" asks Major Morley.

"Yon limmer!" exclaims Mrs. Loudon scornfully. "How can she show her face in any civilised place?"

"There's not much of her face to be seen. I doubt whether her best friend would know her if she washed the paint off."

"There's the bride!" exclaims Mrs. Loudon.

"But no groom in sight," replies Major Morley. "Now that she's got him safely married there's no need for any further effort, I suppose."

I find this kind of duet somewhat boring, and am not sorry when Major Morley and I are discovered by a tennis enthusiast, and invited to make up a four. We find ourselves partnered against Guthrie and Elsie Baker, and proceed to beat them without much difficulty, thanks to Major Morley's slashing service and brilliant returns. Guthrie is a sound player, and puts up a good fight, but his partner is too busy showing off her stylish strokes (most of which go out) to be of much help to him.

It is all very pleasant. The sun shines brightly, and the dresses, though slightly out-of-date according to London standards, look very pretty and gay on the green lawns amongst the flowers.

After the set we are joined by the son of the house, Hector MacQuill. He is very tall, with aquiline features and beautiful hands. Major Morley seems to know him well, and enquires with his usual lack of ceremony how on earth that awful Baker girl got here.

"She *is* rather awful," says young MacQuill. "I've never seen her before. Guthrie Loudon wanted her asked."

"Good God!" says Major Morley. "I spend my whole time avoiding her — she's staying at the Hotel, and she makes eyes at everything in trousers."

"You should wear a kilt," suggests Hector, smiling.

It is now decreed that Mrs. Christie must really see the chapel, and, Mrs. Christie professing herself enchanted to see anything she is shown, arrangements are instantly made for the expedition. Major Morley says Mrs. Loudon should see it too, and, this being agreed upon unanimously, he proposes to fetch the lady in question, and follow us with all speed.

Hector MacQuill and I start off down a mossy path by the side of the river and, after a few minutes' walk, we come upon a ruined chapel overgrown with ivy and surrounded by the gravestones of the MacQuills. I find my guide very interesting, and well-informed regarding the history and habits of his ancestors. He makes them real to me. Their strange barbaric form of life, and the mixture of simplicity and ferocity in their natures are easily understood in the wild setting of frowning crags and dashing river where the tale is told.

"I was named after the wildest of the lot," he says, with a friendly smile which lights up his austere countenance in a remarkable way. "Hector MacQuill was famous for his audacity in an age when audacity was the natural order of things. He was the hero of a hundred fights, and his raids were the most daring in the whole countryside. One day when Hector was out hunting he happened to see MacArbin's daughter, and fell in love with her at first sight. The MacArbins are our hereditary enemies, Mrs. Christie. We are still at daggers drawn with them for no reason but the old feud. You will hardly believe such a thing can *be* in the twentieth century, but my father holds fast to the old traditions. He would as soon pull down the old chapel as give up his ancient enmity with the clan MacArbin. I'm hoping to alter all that, but it won't be easy.

"Well, to return to Hector — it was a sort of Montague and Capulet affair, but Hector was less civilised than Romeo and — shall we say? — more

virile. One dark night he called the clan together, and
made a raid on Castle Darroch (the stronghold of the
MacArbins), carrying off his lady-love from under her
father's nose. He kept her a prisoner at Castle Quill
until she consented to marry him, and then he married
her with splendour and feasting such as had never been
seen in the memory of man. It was a strange wooing,
but the strangest thing was that they were very happy
together, and Seónaid MacArbin became a staunch
MacQuill. Here are their graves, close together beside
this holly bush."

We look at the two little mounds in silence. For my
part I am enthralled with the story, caught back to
those strange wild days where love and war went hand
in hand.

"Hector was a wild devil," continued his namesake.
"He was the terror of the countryside — always up to
some mischief or other. Perhaps you think it strange
that we should be proud of him?"

"He was a man," I reply.

"The MacArbins got him at last. They laid many
traps for him, but Hector seemed to lead a charmed
life. Perhaps he got careless in the end."

"What happened?"

He laughs. "I don't want to bore you, Mrs. Christie."

"It's thrilling," I tell him.

"Well, Hector was out hunting with some of the clan.
Suddenly they heard a woman screaming for help.
Hector called a halt. You can imagine the little band in
the depths of the forest, looking at each other and
wondering what was afoot. The screams came again,

and, without more ado, Hector led the way in the direction from whence they came. They were getting near to the MacArbin stronghold, and some of them must have felt a qualm of fear, for the feud was very fierce, and they could expect no mercy were their enemies to find them on MacArbin territory. But Hector did not know what fear was, he pressed on, and soon they came to a small clearing in the forest, and saw a girl bound to a tree with ropes. She called out that she had been robbed and ill-treated and besought them to loose her. The band were filled with fury at the outrage; they dismounted, and Hector cut her bonds. Scarcely had he done so when the MacArbin battle cry rang out, and a hundred of the MacArbin clan burst through the undergrowth, and fell upon the MacQuills tooth and nail. It was an ambush; Hector had walked into it blindfold.

"The MacQuills, totally unprepared for the onslaught, were soon defeated. Hector was taken, and only two of the band escaped to bring the news to Castle Quill. Next morning Hector's body, full of wounds, and mutilated almost beyond recognition, was found on the road near the Castle gate. They had a grisly sense of humour in those days.

"Seónaid MacQuill was not the woman to take such an insult lying down. She determined to revenge his death. Calling the clan together, she delivered an impassioned address, reminding them of the prowess of their late chief in battle, and his kindness to them in troublous times, and asking for volunteers for certain death. The clan volunteered as one man. Seónaid chose a dozen of the stoutest, and laid before them her plan. That very night, when the MacArbins were celebrating the death of their enemy with wine and feasting, Seónaid led her chosen band into Castle Darroch by a secret passage from the loch. She was a MacArbin, of course — that was how she knew of its existence. When the feast was at its height, Seónaid, with a dozen fierce warriors armed to the teeth, sprang into the banqueting hall and laid about them with their claymores. They were overpowered in the end, and every man of them slain, but not before they had done a good deal of damage amongst their unarmed and unsuspecting hosts. Seónaid herself was killed in the mêlée. I think she intended that this should happen, for she was devoted to Hector, and life without him must have seemed impossible.

"The MacArbins had a custom of throwing the bodies of their dead into the loch upon which their Castle stands. It saved burial, and, truth to tell, there is very little ground round the place where you could dig for three feet without coming upon solid rock. For some unknown reason Loch-an-Darroch never gives up its dead. Nothing thrown into the loch is ever seen again. I suppose it is something to do with the currents or else because it is very deep.

"Seónaid's marriage with a hated MacQuill had rankled for years in the hearts of the MacArbins. They considered her a traitor to her clan, but she still belonged to them, so they decided to give her a MacArbin funeral. The night was dark; they pushed their boats out from the shore; torches made of pine resin threw a red glow upon the waters. The priest read the burial service and Seónaid's body was committed to the loch. Thus the MacArbins vindicated their honour, and reclaimed their own.

"Next morning some women, going down to the loch to wash clothes, found the body of Seónaid washed up in a little bay where the sand was white and the willows drooped over the water. They rushed up to the Castle, screaming out the news, and in a few moments the whole clan was roused and had trooped down to the water's edge to see for itself whether the impossible and unheard-of had really happened. Yes, there was Seónaid lying on the sand, half in and half out of the water, and the little waves were lapping round her and moving the long strands of her hair — Loch-an-Darroch had given up its prey. A terrified silence fell upon the clan; they looked at each other in horror — what terrible thing did this portend?

"'Throw her back again!' cried some of the hot-heads, but the wiseacres would not hear of such a thing. This was a Sign and a Portent; to throw her back would be to invite disaster.

"It was obvious that the loch would have none of her — or else she would have none of the loch. To throw her back was madness, for her spirit would not rest; it would haunt the Castle and cause endless trouble to the clan. It was therefore decided to carry her back to the MacQuills, so that her spirit, if it felt restless in its narrow bed, might haunt clan MacQuill rather than clan MacArbin.

"So it was that Seónaid had another funeral — slightly more orthodox than her first — and was buried beside Hector in MacQuill ground."

"And does she haunt them?" I ask, for the story has seized upon my imagination, and a ghost would be a fitting and pleasantly creepy sequel.

The modern Hector laughs. "I'm afraid I don't believe in ghosts, Mrs. Christie, but some people are under the impression that they have seen the spirit of Seónaid walking upon Loch-an-Darroch or haunting the ruined Castle of the MacArbins."

"What, have we a Highlander here who doesn't believe in ghosts?" says Mrs. Loudon. She and Major Morley have approached us while we were talking, and have overheard the last words of the story.

"Have you told Mrs. Christie about the bard?" enquires Major Morley.

"I think I've told her enough for one day," replies Hector MacQuill with a laugh; but I am determined to hear all I can, and after a little persuasion he continues. "In those days there was no written record of events, but every clan had a bard (or poet) who composed verses, commemorating the brave doings of his chief, and set them to music. These songs were handed down from father to son, and, in this way, some record was kept. The bard belonging to clan MacQuill composed an ode to Seónaid, and it is through this ode that the story I have told you has travelled down the centuries to the present day. Of course the poem was in Gaelic, but the last part might be translated something like this:

"In dark Loch-an-Darroch, beneath the stark
  crags,
Our Seónaid found no rest.
How should MacQuill sleep in MacArbin water?
How should a lioness find peace in the lair of a
  badger?
Would the proud eagle who nests on Ben Seoch
Seek shelter in the pigeon-house?
Seónaid was ours from the day when we took
  her,
Our courage and cunning won her from our foes.
Brave Hector bore her home upon his black
  steed,
And the skies flashed and thundered.
Lovely as the night was Seónaid —
Her hair floated upon the waters of Darroch,
Like a black cloud it floated round her,
And like a water-lily was her face.
She came back from the grave,
And brought fear to the black hearts of
  MacArbin.
They looked upon her and trembled.
Take her up and bring her safely home,
To her true home by the dashing river Quill,
Which comes down from Ben Seoch like a lion
  seeking its prey,
And all who drink of it are filled with courage.
Bring her home to her own people who loved her
  well.
Lay her down gently in the kindly warm earth.

65

Hector the brave, and Seónaid the beautiful —
Together they sleep in the shade of the holly."

None of us speaks for a moment or two, and perhaps
this is the right tribute to pay.

"Do you think she really was very beautiful?" Major
Morley asks at last.

"I think she was," replies Hector. "The MacArbin
women have all been noted for their beauty, and
Seónaid was the same type — pale as a lily, with dark
hair — oh yes, she was certainly beautiful."

"How quiet it is here!" says Mrs. Loudon. "Even the
river seems to run softly past this place, as if it were
afraid of disturbing their rest."

"They had a wild time while it lasted," Major Morley
says. "They've earned a peaceful sleep. I think I should
have liked to live in those days —"

"What! — with no hot baths, Tony?" asks Hector
MacQuill, smiling.

"That would be a drawback, of course," replies
Major Morley, gravely. "But think how pleasant to be
able to kill off your enemies whenever you felt inclined
— unless, of course, they got you first — and if you
fancied anybody as a wife you just carried her off and
married her. On the whole we have lost more than we
have gained by the march of civilisation."

"Isn't there a salmon loup near here?" asks Mrs.
Loudon, looking round her as if she expects to see
salmon leaping amongst the trees.

"Yes, there is," replies Hector MacQuill. "Why not
walk down the river and have a look at it? Of course,

there will be no salmon going up — October is the best month to see the salmon — but the falls are very pretty, and, anyway, it is a better occupation on a hot day than hitting a ball about in the sun. I shall have to go back to my duties as host. I'm afraid I have been away from them too long already — but Tony knows the way."

I have never seen a "salmon loup," and am delighted at the prospect of adding to my experiences — even if there are no salmon on view. At the back of my mind there lingers a faint hope that we might see one, foolish enough to have made a mistake in the date.

The three of us, therefore, bid a temporary farewell to our host, and stroll down the little path amongst feathery grasses, shaded from the sun by a canopy of tall trees.

The sound of falling water comes to our ears, at first faintly like the sound of the distant sea, but with every step it grows louder and louder, until our ears are filled with the thunder of it, and we see the river, which has hitherto kept us company, disappear over a rocky precipice, and fall in several green billows, broken by rocks and fringed with foam, into a dark pool some twenty feet below.

Major Morley seizes my arm, and we climb over the rocks and watch the falling water for a long time without speaking. Indeed the sound of the falls is too loud for conversation to be possible. I am dazed and mesmerised with the noise, and quite glad to cling to my companion's arm.

How beautiful it is! How wild and primeval! There is something almost terrifying in the relentless way the river flings itself over its barrier of rock and plunges down amongst flying spray and creamy foam. The spray is full of rainbows, and drops of rainbow hue sparkle upon the feathery fronds of the ferns which overhang the pool.

"A lot of water to-day," shouts Major Morley. "Melting snow — Ben Seoch —"

I wish he would be quiet and not try to talk. It is enough for me to watch the curling billows, and the rainbow spray — I don't want to know where it comes from — I could stand here all day just looking at it —

But Major Morley is tugging at my arm, and I realise that we have been here long enough, and it is time for tea.

We are bound with chains of iron to this strange custom of eating and drinking at set hours, whether we want to eat and drink or not. With unwilling feet I follow my companions up the path. Their conversation — which I can now overhear in snatches — is evidently a continuation of one started before, and appears to be on the subject of Elsie Baker.

Mrs. Loudon has found, not only a sympathetic ear in Major Morley, but a fellow sufferer who is prepared to go even farther than herself in the vilification of the wretched girl. I have purposely refrained from criticising Elsie Baker to Mrs. Loudon, because I feel in my bones that Guthrie intends to marry her, and probably will, unless something unforeseen occurs. Major Morley has no such scruples — he lays bare her manifold delinquencies before Mrs. Loudon's horrified eyes. According to Major Morley she is a cocktail drinker, a cigarette fiend, and a man-hunter. He says that she lies in wait for him in the corridor, bumps into him on purpose, and then screams with pretended fear. He says that her plucked eyebrows give him shivers all down his back, and her golden hair sets his teeth on edge. He says that her lips and the tips of her fingers remind him of a cannibal after a meal of raw flesh —

Mrs. Loudon's eyes nearly fall out of their sockets. "What a like creature for a daughter-in-law!" she exclaims.

"Oh, come now, it's not as bad as all that," says Major Morley. "Sailors often fall for impossible women."

"And marry them," adds Mrs. Loudon with impenetrable gloom.

"I can't believe that *your son* —" Major Morley hints with flattering emphasis.

Even this compliment fails to raise the lady's spirits. "The man's bereft of his senses," she replies trenchantly.

"Something must be done about it," says Major Morley gravely. "It simply can't be allowed. Surely between us we can think of a plan to rescue this poor deluded man."

Mrs. Loudon brightens a little. "Major Morley! The creature is staying at your hotel. Couldn't you —"

"Nothing doing, I assure you," says Major Morley, laughing. "Not even for your son would I allow myself to fall into her clutches. Besides, it would be a fatal mistake. It would only make him all the keener if he saw another victim in her toils. No, there's a much better way than that — but I should need Mrs. Christie's help."

"Why, of course Hester will help you!" cries Mrs. Loudon, full of excitement at the prospect of something to be done.

I look at him doubtfully; he is so difficult to understand, such a queer mixture of kindness and wickedness. What mood is he in at the present moment? I rather think he is enjoying himself, in spite of his grave countenance and sympathetic manner.

"It's quite simple," says Major Morley, leading us to a garden seat which stands conveniently near. "Let's sit down for a few minutes and discuss the matter fully. You need not be alarmed, Mrs. Christie. All you have to do is to look charming and allow me to adore you from afar. The first is natural to you already, the second will come quite naturally in time."

"But I don't see what good that will do," I protest; for, to tell the truth, I don't like the plan at all.

"Surely, you see," says Major Morley, persuasively. "Our friend Guthrie sees me adoring, and takes one glance at Mrs. Christie — he has not seen her before, because he is blinded by his infatuation for his cannibal — one glance at Mrs. Christie is enough, he will never look at Miss Baker again."

The plan seems to me the height of foolishness, and I say so firmly. But Mrs. Loudon — who seems bewitched out of her usual sanity — is attracted by the idea, and beseeches me to "try it," pointing out that at any rate it can do no harm. It is really Mrs. Loudon's own original plan, only carried to insane lengths.

70

"I'm not so sure about its harmlessness," I reply.

"Why?" asks Mrs. Loudon. "What harm can it do?"

Major Morley seconds her by pointing out that I need do nothing. *He* will do all that is necessary. And adds, that surely I can bear to be adored from afar to save a poor young man from the clutches of a cannibal.

I feel certain that Tim would object to the plan, but all my arguments are overruled or swept aside by my companions. They settle everything to their entire satisfaction — though not to mine — and we return to the garden, where we find the sacred rites of afternoon tea are being celebrated with suitable solemnity.

"I'm afraid you will have to call me 'Tony,'" Major Morley says gravely, as he appears at my side with a cup of tea and a plate of cream buns. "It's rather a nuisance for you, of course, but we want to make the thing as real as possible, and there is no time to lose — poor 'froggy' is fast hooked, I'm afraid."

"Froggy?" I enquire.

"He would a-wooing go, whether his mother would let him or no," explains Major Morley. "There is the poor wight, holding a lace parasol for the Cannibal Queen — and very silly he looks."

I glance in the direction indicated, and see that it is only too true. Guthrie is making a fool of himself.

"He's hardly worth rescuing, is he?" remarks my companion, guessing my thoughts in an uncanny way he has.

Mrs. Loudon has been claimed by an old crony, so we find a seat in the shade, and Major Morley (or Tony, as I suppose I must call him) sits down at my feet, and

71

gazes at me with a yearning expression which is so realistic that it makes me feel quite uncomfortable.

Presently Guthrie appears, and asks if I will make up a four.

"Don't tire yourself, Hester," says Tony anxiously. "I really think you are more comfortable sitting here in the shade with me." But I have had quite enough of sitting in the shade with Tony, and profess myself quite ready for a game. Tony jumps up with alacrity, and says in that case he will play too, and we can have a return of our previous set. This does not appeal to Guthrie at all (he is not very fond of being beaten and he is quite aware that he and Elsie are not strong enough for us). He suggests that we should "split up," but Tony insists on playing with me. All Guthrie's feeble objections are countered — he is no match for Tony in diplomacy — and, a court falling vacant at the critical moment, we take them on again and beat them worse than before.

Guthrie's patience wears somewhat thin during the set, and he points out to his partner that her spectacular strokes are losing them every game. To which Elsie replies that her forehand drive has been much admired by Mr. Jones, the professional at her club in Portsmouth. At this exchange of pleasantries Tony winks at me, and serves an easy lob to Elsie, which she promptly drives, with all her force, into the back net. This gives us the set.

It is now time to go. Tony rushes off to find our car, and packs us into it with anxious care — he is extraordinarily good at these small attentions. "I may call?" he enquires of Mrs. Loudon, as he tucks the rug round her feet.

"Of course — any friend of Hester's. Come over to-morrow afternoon," she murmurs hospitably.

Guthrie, who has elected to drive, starts the car with a jerk that nearly upsets Tony — the latter still having one foot on the step — and we career madly over the drawbridge, and down the drive, which is now crowded with departing guests.

"For any sake take care!" exclaims Mrs. Loudon in a surprised voice. "You nearly had the kilt off that man, Guthrie."

"The damned fool should keep off the road," replies Guthrie murderously. From all of which I deduce that the good Guthrie is slightly put out about something.

TUESDAY: 7TH JUNE

SNOW-WHITE AND THE SEVEN DWARFS — TONY TALKS TO MRS. FALCONER — OUR ADVENTURE WITH BURGLARS

Annie has gone into the village on some mysterious errand that only she herself can do, so Betty and I take our favourite book of fairy-tales into the garden.

"Read about Snow-White and the Seven Dwarfs," says Betty. "You read much nicer than Annie. I like when you make them talk with different voices, Mummie."

We spread a rug under a fir tree and settle down.

At this moment there is a glimpse of a blue frock at the gate in the fence leading to the woods, and Guthrie hurries down the garden and leaps the burn. He has gone to meet her, of course. They must have arranged to meet, and go for a walk together — now we know why Guthrie was so *distrait* at lunch-time, and why he threw cold water on all his mother's suggestions for spending the afternoon.

Meanwhile the book has opened conveniently at the picture of Snow-White in her glass coffin, which must always be thoroughly examined before the story begins. "Don't the dwarfs look sad?" Betty says in sympathetic

74

tones. "Of course they don't know she'll come to life again when the coffin gets banged against a tree. How hard could you bang a glass coffin against a tree without it breaking, Mummie?" she enquires interestedly.

Like most of Betty's questions this is difficult to answer, so I suggest we should begin the story.

"Yes, begin," says Betty, with a luxurious sigh.

" 'Once upon a time there was a beautiful queen — ' "

So we set off together on the well-known journey with the little princess whose skin was as white as snow, and whose cheeks were as red as the rose. Betty listens, enthralled, while the wicked Queen tries to poison her beautiful stepdaughter with a poisoned comb, and to choke her with a magic apple. Custom cannot stale the thrill of the story for Betty, she knows it by heart, yet her eyes gleam with excitement and her small body is gathered into a tense ball.

"And what are they doing now?" I wonder to myself, for long practice has made it possible for me to think my own thoughts and read quite easily at the same time. The two threads mingle and commingle in a single strand. Snow-White strays through the dark woods with Guthrie and Elsie Baker, their fates seem bound together, and flow along in one melodious stream. The little dwarfs peer at them from behind the trees, and consult together in their strange gruff voices as to what had better be done about it all. And how I wish these same little dwarfs would cease their useless labour of making a glass coffin for Snow-White, and would rush after Guthrie and Elsie, and tear them apart! They are fitted for each other in no way that I can see, and, instead of growing together, they will grow apart. Guthrie is grave, with a taste for fantastic humour which Elsie will never appreciate; Elsie is frivolous and enjoys the society of frivolous people. They will hate each other's friends, and misunderstand each other's wit. What hope is there for them?

I sit on by myself long after the story is finished, and Betty has flown off to the garden to find Donald and pester him for gooseberries. The tale of Snow-White is finished, but the tale of Guthrie is still to be told. How sad it is to see a tale marred in the making! Why must we stand aside and see those we care for heading straight for shipwreck on the rocks of life?

I have become very fond of Guthrie in the last few days — there is something lovable in his very simplicity. I can see his faults, of course, but they are offset by his virtues. How strange are the differences in people! Guthrie is boyish, almost childlike in nature; his sulkiness is short-lived, his selfishness is the selfishness of a child. The sun shines through him, and his every thought is mirrored on his open countenance. And Tony Morley is like a deep pool whose bottom you cannot see for the darkness of the water — not muddy water, not that kind of opaqueness, but clear dark water that reflects here a rock, there a patch of blue sky with a passing cloud — and the ripples play over the surface with every breath of wind.

I gaze up at the fir tree above my head, and admire its light green frills, which are sewn on to its dark green frock with invisible stitches — light green frills moving up and down gently in the faintly stirring air — while, with another part of my mind, I dissect the differences in these two men. Guthrie is this, Tony is that, I like Guthrie for this, I like Tony for that. Thoughts flicker about me quickly, vaguely, so that my brain, lulled to drowsiness by the afternoon peace, cannot follow them. They dance up and down before my eyes like a cloud of midges — up and down — up and down.

Take Tony first. How considerate he is! How quick to respond to an idea! How sensitive to other people's feelings! Yes, but sometimes he tramples on them on purpose (which Guthrie never does), and isn't it worse to trample purposely than to trample unconsciously, like Guthrie? — like a huge elephant in the jungle, leaving a track of broken flowers in its wake . . .

"Are you asleep, Hester?" Mrs. Loudon says, and I think I must have been, for Guthrie had turned into an elephant, and was standing trumpeting fiercely at his reflection in a dark pool — and the dark pool was rippling softly as if it were smiling to itself.

"Major Morley's come," continues my hostess. "He's talking to Millie in the drawing-room — or perhaps it would be more like the thing to say that Millie's talking to him. I thought we'd have tea early, and you can take him fishing. Where's Guthrie?"

I rub my eyes and try to banish the mists which are still clouding my brain —

77

"Poor lassie — you're half asleep yet. I'd not have wakened you, but I can't leave the Major in Millie's clutches — the man will be deaved to death."

"You needn't worry about *him*," I reply, trying to smooth my hair, which seems to be standing straight on end. "Major Morley is quite capable of looking after himself."

"Come away," she adjures me impatiently. "The man's come to see *you*, not to listen to Millie's haverings."

I follow my hostess meekly towards the drawing-room windows which open on to the veranda. We pause outside and look at each other in bewilderment, for it is Major Morley's voice, and not Mrs. Falconer's, which comes clearly to our ears.

"Father always insisted that us boys should come home for the Christmas holidays," he says in confidential tones. "Sometimes we begged him to allow us to stay at school and continue our studies, but father wouldn't hear of it. 'You *must* have two helpings of plum pudding on Christmas Day,' he used to say. 'And how can I be sure that you eat it unless I have you under my own eye?' Well, one Christmas holidays a very strange thing happened — it may have been in the year 1900 or 1901, or possibly 1902. I remember distinctly that it was a Monday, because we had had cold beef for lunch (but you must not think it was anything to do with the cold beef; cold beef may be indigestible, but it does not predispose a person to hallucinations). It must have been about half past three in the afternoon, because I was just beginning to feel hungry for tea, and it was probably a few days after Christmas, because my young cousin had been given a new pair of footer boots and was busy rubbing them with castor oil — castor oil has such a filthy smell," adds Tony thoughtfully.

"Yes, but what —"

"Suddenly," says Tony, interrupting the poor lady unmercifully. "Suddenly there were footsteps on the gravel outside the open window — it was an old man coming up the drive with a sack over his back, or it may have been a woman selling bootlaces, or an Italian boy selling onions, or a Punch-and-Judy man — the fact is, it was really too dark to see who it was, which shows it must have been a very dark afternoon, shouldn't you say so, Mrs. Falconer?"

Mrs. Falconer says, "But if you couldn't see who it was —"

"Ah, but I could smell the onions," replies Tony triumphantly. "And that proves conclusively that it must have been an Italian onion-boy, because if it had been a Punch-and-Judy man he would have smelt of whisky — there was a Punch-and-Judy man who used to come round quite often during the holidays; he had a very red nose, poor fellow, and his breath always smelt of whisky — and bootlaces have a peculiar smell of their own, so it couldn't possibly have been the bootlace woman."

"Papa always used to say —" Mrs. Falconer begins, seizing her opportunity while her opponent pauses for breath.

"And he was perfectly right," agrees Tony earnestly. "Bootlaces are not what they were. I've never met a

79

modern bootlace that could stand a good tug. And studs — the way they leap into corners and hide under mats! It's my belief, Mrs. Falconer, that all studs are possessed of an evil spirit, and I simply don't believe these fellows who write to the papers saying that they have used the same stud for thirty years. The thing's impossible. I once knew a man who was completely ruined by a stud —"

"Ruined by a stud!" gasps Mrs. Falconer.

"Don't ask me to tell you about it." Tony says, with a slight tremble in his voice. "The man was my friend — you will be the first to admit that silence is golden. Let us talk of shoes, or ships, or sealing-wax — I know a fellow who uses pink sealing-wax — a most disgusting habit! This man actually had the impertinence to write a proposal of marriage to a lady he had known for nine days — or it may have been nine years, I really can't remember which, and it doesn't matter, for both are equally insulting, you will agree. In nine days he couldn't possibly have known her well enough to propose, and in nine years he should have known her too well. But the point is he sealed the letter with pink sealing-wax, which warned the poor girl in the nick of time. She was good enough to ask my advice on the subject. 'Shall I accept him, Tony?' she said to me with tears in her eyes. 'Shall I accept him, and spend my life trying to wean him from his vicious habits?' But, alas, I could give her no hope! I knew, only too well, that a man can never be broken of pink sealing-wax, once it has a hold on him."

"But surely you don't mean —"

80

"No, no!" says Tony gravely. "You must not think I meant *that*. Let us leave the subject and go on to cabbages. Personally I would rather eat hay or thistles, but I am told that quite a number of people consider the cabbage fit for human consumption. The hard-hearted ones are best — they are tougher, and have more white stalk to the cubic inch."

"Dear Papa did not care for cabbage," Mrs. Falconer announces breathlessly.

"Of course not!" exclaims Tony with rapture. "Nobody did. It is only recently that the cabbage has come to the fore. In your father's time a gentleman ate to please his palate; nowadays he eats to pamper his stomach. Do not blush, Mrs. Falconer. I assure you that this important organ may now be spoken of with impunity in the drawing-rooms of Mayfair. However, if you would rather go on to kings, you have only to say the word. It is the last subject on our list, but by no means the least worthy of exploration. Which is *your* favourite king? Mine has always been Charles the Second. I feel that he and I would have hit it off splendidly. For many years I found myself in the minority on this point, but I am glad to notice a distinct revulsion in his favour amongst thinking men and women. Why, only the other day the Y.W.C.A. had an exhibition of his relics! It is not a body in which one would expect to find appreciation of the Merry Monarch — but, after all, why not? Doubtless he gave pleasure to a great many young women who would otherwise have led somewhat drab lives —"

At this moment Mrs. Loudon sneezes violently, and discovers our presence. The monologue ceases abruptly.

"There you are," says Tony. "Mrs. Falconer and I have had a most interesting conversation — the time has simply flown."

Mrs. Falconer says nothing; there is a dazed look in her eyes.

"We must really continue our conversation some time," Tony says brazenly, as we take our places round the tea-table. "We have not exhausted the subject of kings."

"Perhaps you have exhausted Mrs. Falconer," I suggest maliciously.

"Cruel!" he sighs, helping himself to a scone.

Guthrie's chair looks very empty — there are several other unoccupied chairs in the room, but only Guthrie's looks empty. I remark on the phenomenon, but nobody seems to get my point.

"Where *is* Guthrie?" enquires his mother, a trifle anxiously. "Have any of you seen him this afternoon?"

Tony says that he saw Guthrie and Miss Thingummy starting off for a walk, but he doesn't suppose they've gone far. When asked the reason for his supposition, he replies that people *don't* as a rule. They generally sit down on the first thing handy.

Mrs. Loudon sighs heavily, and Mrs. Falconer, somewhat revived by a cup of strong tea, whispers to me, "Do you think he's offered for her yet?" but I pretend not to hear.

After tea Tony and I go out on the loch together. Tony insists on acting as boatman, and gives me some valuable advice on the art of throwing a fly. I catch several fine trout, and enjoy myself thoroughly.

Tony is really much more unselfish than most men — or else he is not such a keen fisherman, or else — But there is no other explanation; he can't be such a keen fisherman.

About seven o'clock the breeze freshens, and Tony says we had better pack up now, it's too cold for me. I point out that he need not keep up the pretence of solicitude for my welfare when Guthrie is not here to see it, whereupon Tony replies that it is excellent practice for him, and rows firmly homewards.

We find Guthrie waiting for us at the boathouse. He seems slightly out of temper, and says he has been waiting for nearly an hour, and didn't we hear him shouting to us. (Now that I think of it I believe I did hear somebody shouting.)

Tony replies that the wind is in the other direction, and anyhow it is too cold to fish any more to-night.

"Cold!" snorts Guthrie. "I don't call it cold. Some people seem to be made of cotton wool."

Tony takes no notice of this strange remark; he busies himself collecting the fishing tackle, and making fast the boat.

"What about another hour's fishing?" Guthrie says, ignoring Tony, and addressing himself to me in a wheedling manner. "Dinner isn't till eight, you know, Hester."

I am about to reply when Tony says innocently, "I suppose there is a ghillie belonging to the place, isn't there, Loudon? Or do you depend entirely on your guests to work the boat for you?"

Guthrie opens his mouth to reply, but no sound comes. He watches in silence while Tony helps me out of the boat as if I were made of spun glass (this is for his especial benefit, of course) and we all walk up to the house together.

Mrs. Loudon comes into my room when I am going to bed and says THE PLAN is working admirably. Guthrie has just been advising her not to ask that fellow Morley to the house any more "as he seems rather gone on Hester." Whereupon I tell her flatly that I hate the plan and everything to do with it, and that I don't know what on earth Tim would say if he knew.

Mrs. Loudon replies, incoherently, that it would do Tim a lot of good, and that he will never know anything about it, and that anyway I'm not doing anything wrong. "And anyway I've asked the man to come over to-morrow afternoon," she adds firmly, "and I'll not put him off for all Guthrie's blethering."

She stays a few moments longer, talking about various matters, and then goes away.

I suppose I must have gone to sleep at once, for I seem to have been asleep for hours — but quite suddenly, I am wide awake. It is raining hard and quite dark. Perhaps it is the heavy rain that has wakened me. I lie very still and listen.

Somebody is on the veranda beneath my window. I can hear the sound of hushed voices, and the pad of stealthy feet on the tiles. The sounds are the more alarming because there have been several small burglaries lately in the neighbourhood, and I decide at once that the correct thing for me to do is to waken Guthrie. I slip on my dressing-gown in the dark, and grope my way along the passage to his room. How dark it is! It must be about midnight, for dawn comes early in these latitudes.

Guthrie is fast asleep, but he wakes quickly, and takes in the situation without loss of time.

"Gosh!" he exclaims excitedly. "They've come to the wrong house this time. I must put on my boots — you can't go after burglars without boots."

I point out that Guthrie's boots will make the most frightful noise on the uncarpeted stairs, and that by the time he has reached the bottom the burglars will have gone. After arguing obstinately for a few moments we compromise on tennis shoes. He dons a cardigan, and an overcoat — I never knew a man who could start to do anything without dressing for the part — and, opening the drawer of his dressing-table, produces a small revolver, examines the chamber carefully, and slips it into his pocket. I begin to feel quite sorry for the burglars. A pocket torch completes our outfit. This is given into my charge with instructions to "flash it into their eyes." Guthrie will then wing them, tie them up with rope, and gag them with old socks — here the socks are produced and tucked into my dressing-gown pocket.

"By the way, Hester," he says anxiously, "I suppose there is some washing-rope or something in the house — if not we shall have to make do with blind-cord."

It all sounds quite easy.

Guthrie continues that, after having bound them securely, we shall lock them up in the coal-cellar, and rouse Dobbie, and send him off to Inverquill for the police. It's most important to have all your plans cut and dried beforehand, Guthrie says, and then you know exactly where you are. If Jellicoe had been able to do this at Jutland we should have bagged the whole German Fleet. I am suitably impressed by this statement, and follow Guthrie downstairs. It is very cold, and the rain is still coming down hard. I hear it swishing on the cupola with an eerie sound. My teeth show an impulse to chatter — I rather wish I had put on some warm stockings, and a jumper, but it is too late now.

We look in the pantry first, Guthrie explaining, in a hoarse whisper, that of course the burglars know where the silver is kept. They never undertake a job of this kind without obtaining a plan of the house. He thinks the garden-boy may have given it to them — he's a shifty-looking individual — or that man who came to look at the kitchen range.

There are no signs of burglars in the pantry — everything is in apple-pie order, and as quiet as the grave — the dining-room is also innocent of their presence. We look carefully under the table and into various cupboards. Guthrie says they might have heard us coming and hidden themselves.

I point out to Guthrie that it was on the veranda outside the drawing-room window I heard them, so the inference is that they are in the drawing-room, making a clean sweep of Mrs. Loudon's cherished snuff-boxes and silver photograph frames. Guthrie replies that it is better to look elsewhere first, but can give no good reason for his statement, and I begin to wonder whether he is really very keen to meet them now that the time has come. I do not like to question the courage of an officer in His Majesty's Navy, but this is my impression.

We have now looked everywhere except in the drawing-room, and there is no further excuse for delay. We listen outside the door and hear the sound of whispering — or else it may be the rain.

Suddenly Guthrie throws open the door and enters, revolver in hand. I flash the torch in their faces, and the tableau is revealed.

The burglars consist of a tall man in a check overcoat, and a girl in a burberry, with a green tammy on the back of her head. They have lighted one candle, but its fitful flame throws scarcely any light upon the scene.

"Hello, Loudon!" the man says. "Cleared for action, I see."

"Good God!" Guthrie exclaims. "What on earth are you doing here, Bones?"

I realise at once that this tall, thin, lanky individual must be a friend of Guthrie's — or perhaps it would be exaggerating to say a *friend*, for Guthrie does not seem enchanted to see him.

"What on earth brought you here at this time of night?" he asks again, in the irritable tone of one who has been thoroughly frightened and finds his bogy innocuous.

"An Austin Seven brought us here," replies the man addressed as Bones, with a nonchalant air. "Found you'd all cleared off to bed, so we thought we'd warm ourselves a bit — damned cold outside, and wet too."

"See here, I guess you'd better introduce us, Bones," says the girl suddenly, "and then we can get what we want and hook it. Your pal doesn't seem overjoyed to see us — I guess we must have woke him out of his beauty sleep. Say," she adds, turning to me, "you don't happen to have a baby's bottle, do you?"

I reply in a dazed manner that I have not. It flashes through my mind that they must have escaped from a lunatic asylum; perhaps the ropes may still be required.

Bones now perceives me in the gloom. "Good Lord!" he exclaims. "Didn't know you were married, Loudon. Won't you introduce me to your wife? Wouldn't have come, I assure you, if I'd known about it. When did it happen, old man? Congratulations and all that — hope we didn't pop in at an inopportune moment?"

"I'm *not* married," Guthrie says indignantly.

"Even sorrier, then," says Bones, eyeing me with increased interest.

"Look here, I wish you'd say what you want and go," Guthrie says inhospitably. "This is Mrs. Christie — she's staying here with my mother —"

Bones takes this as a formal introduction, and bows gracefully.

88

"I don't know what on earth you want," Guthrie continues. "But *I* want to get back to bed."

"Don't wonder," murmurs Bones. "Don't wonder at all, old chap. I'd feel the same myself. By the way, you couldn't produce a spot, I suppose. Dry work this treasure hunting."

"You've had quite enough," says the girl firmly. "You've got to drive that car back to Inverquill to-night."

"Lord! I've not begun," replies Bones. "You should see what I can take without rocking — I can still say Irish Constabulary without a hitch."

"Did you come here for a drink?" enquires Guthrie.

"Well, not exactly — still a spot never comes amiss —" suggests Bones hopefully.

"I guess you'd better explain — or let me," says the girl. "See here, Mr. — er — (Bones didn't say what your name was). This is the way of it — Bones and I are in a treasure hunt — we're staying over at Inverquill, with the MacKenzies. Well, Bones and I are in the last lap, and we're just mad to win, so —"

"Had a gin and bitters at Avielochan Hotel," says the lanky man, taking up the tale. "Suddenly remembered you were here — wonderful how a gin and bitters stimulates a fellow — took us hours to find you — but here we are."

"So I see," says Guthrie unpleasantly.

"You'll help us, won't you!" says the girl, producing a printed list, somewhat damp and crumpled, from her waterproof pocket. "I guess we've got nearly everything

89

now, except a baby's bottle, and a warming-pan, and a poker —"

"Here's a poker," Bones says, seizing the one out of the grate.

"You're not going to take that poker," says Guthrie suddenly.

"Bring it back to-morrow, old man," Bones replies, trying to stuff it into his pocket.

The girl continues to consult the list anxiously, holding it near the solitary candle. I perceive that it is she who is the moving spirit in the treasure hunt. Bones is but lukewarm.

"Look here, Bones," says Guthrie, with a sudden access of rage. "You put that poker back in its place, and clear out of here — I'm just about fed up with this nonsense."

"Make it a deoch an doruis and I'm your man," replies Bones quickly. "One small one, and out we go. You couldn't turn a dog out without a drink on a night like this."

Perhaps Guthrie thinks that this is the quickest way to get rid of the man. At any rate he relents.

"All right," he says ungraciously. "You'll get a small one and you'll clear out. Hester, you had better go back to bed, you'll get your death of cold. I'll see these lunatics off the premises."

I realise that I am almost frozen, and am quite glad to take Guthrie's advice — besides, the fun is over. I grope my way upstairs, and creep into bed with my dressing-gown on — thank goodness there is still a little warmth in my hot-water bottle. My room is turning a soft grey colour, dawn is not far off. I reflect what strange ways people have of enjoying themselves, rushing round the country on a wet dark night collecting baby's bottles and warming-pans.

It is some little while before I hear our burglars departing. Guthrie seems to have some trouble with the lock of the door on to the veranda, then I hear his tennis shoes come padding up the stairs and along the passage. He stops at my door and knocks gently.

"What happened?" I enquire.

The door half opens, and Guthrie's head appears. "Are you all right, Hester?" he asks softly. "They've gone at last — I had to give them the poker, and a warming-pan which was hanging in the hall — they wouldn't go away without them."

"You looked as if you wanted to throw them out," I giggled feebly.

"Oh, I'd have thrown Bones out — but I couldn't throw out a girl. Wait till we get back to the *Polyphon*," he adds ferociously. "I'll set the whole ward-room on to him. They hate him as it is, and they'll be only too pleased to make his life a burden — he'll wish he'd never been born when I've done with him — the blinkety, blankety fool!"

In his excitement Guthrie has come into my room, and stands beside my bed, a huge dark-looming figure in the half light.

"I can't help laughing when I think of us and our 'cut and dried' plans," I tell him.

Guthrie says he doesn't see anything funny about it — naturally we thought it was burglars and prepared accordingly.

"Yes, but it wasn't burglars."

"No, it was lunatics."

I can see that Guthrie feels he has been made to look a fool, and does not like it — few men do.

"Look here," he continues, "let's keep the whole thing dark — it's no use worrying Mother by telling *her* about it — she might be nervous if she knew it was so easy to get into the house. Those two just walked in by the veranda door. There's something funny about the lock. Sometimes it locks all right, and sometimes it doesn't."

"Anyone might get in!" I exclaim, sitting up in bed.

"That's just where you're wrong. Nobody would except an ass like Bones. No burglar would ever think of trying the handle of a door. Besides I know now, and I'll make it my business to lock it every night, so you see there's no need to tell Mother."

"She'll miss the poker and the warming-pan."

"Oh, well, we must trust to luck," he says. "You'd better go to sleep; it's nearly dawn."

"I can't go to sleep with you standing there looking like a giant," I announce pettishly.

"Oh no, of course not," he says. "Well, good night, Hester. You won't say anything to Mother, will you?"

I make no reply, except to snuggle down in bed, and he goes away, shutting the door carefully. As a matter of fact I have made up my mind to tell Mrs. Loudon the whole story at the earliest opportunity — she is the last woman to be alarmed at the idea of burglars, and she would thoroughly enjoy the joke.

WEDNESDAY: 8TH JUNE

THE PICNIC AT CASTLE DARROCH —
A GHOST AND A THUNDERSTORM

Guthrie is late in appearing for breakfast, and admits that he did not sleep well. Mrs. Loudon commiserates with him on his insomnia, and says the rain was awful, but she supposes the country needed it, and anyway it was better to rain at night if it had to rain at all.

I wait until I see Guthrie going off with his gun to shoot rabbits, and then track my hostess to her desk.

"Well!" she says, looking up at me. "What happened last night?"

"How did you know that anything happened?" I ask in amazement.

"Circumstantial evidence," she replies, smiling rather strangely. "The warming-pan has vanished from the hall, Guthrie owns to a sleepless night, and a pair of his socks have been discovered in the pocket of your dressing-gown."

I can do nothing but laugh.

"You may laugh," she says. "The whole thing's a mystery to me. I've been trying to unravel it for the last hour."

"You never will."

"No, I dare say not, but there's no need for me to worry my head any more about it since you followed me in here to tell me the whole thing. I could see you were like a cat on hot bricks till you got Guthrie out of the house."

"He said I wasn't to tell you," I reply. "But I made up my mind I would — you will enjoy the joke."

"I'm glad of that," she says, with her twinkle.

Without further ado I embark upon my tale.

Mrs. Loudon follows with interest, and laughs at the right moment; she is an admirable listener. "Well," she says, "I never heard the like of that — the idea of a girl racketing about all night with a man in a car collecting baby's bottles. Mercy me! You're quite right, Hester. I never would have guessed *that*, if I'd spent the rest of my life at it.

"Wait and see what I'll say to Guthrie," she adds, chuckling to herself. "I'll get on to him about this."

"You are not to say a word about it to Guthrie," I tell her firmly. "If you do I'll have nothing more to do with that ridiculous plan of yours and Tony's."

This threat is enough, and she reluctantly consents to spare Guthrie this time. We are still discussing things when a large car drives up to the door, and a wooden-faced chauffeur hands in the warming-pan and the poker. Mrs. Loudon says she is glad to see them, for she would not know how to account for their absence to Mrs. MacRae. We restore them to their rightful places without further comment.

The afternoon being fine and warm, with no suspicion of the all-essential breeze, it is decided to give the fish a holiday, and that the whole party shall take the car for Loch-an-Darroch and picnic there. Everyone assures me that I really must see this loch, and the castle upon its brink, as it is one of the wildest and most beautiful spots in Scotland. Feel suitably excited and impressed.

Tony Morley arrives soon after lunch in his Bentley. Betty greets him rapturously, for they are old friends, and asks if she can sit beside him on the front seat. There is no false pride about my daughter. If she wants a thing she asks for it, and usually attains her desire, very few people having the moral courage to urge their own preferences in the face of her demands. Guthrie and Miss Baker — who is also of the party — elect to travel in the Bentley, which leaves Mrs. Loudon, Mrs. Falconer and myself for the Austin. We squeeze into the back seat, and the picnic baskets are piled up beside Dobbie.

Tony calls out that he will wait for us at the loch, and away goes the Bentley with a scrunch of gravel. Dobbie remarks enviously that they could be there and back before we have started, which is an obvious libel on his mistress's comfortable car. We follow the others at a reasonable pace, cruising along very peacefully over the white roads, and admiring the scenery. Mrs. Loudon is subdued, owing, I feel sure, to the knowledge that Guthrie and Miss Baker are ensconced in the back seat of Tony's car, and therefore at liberty to hold each other's hands without fear of intrusion upon their privacy.

"I suppose Dobbie knows the way," Mrs. Falconer suggests, in a dubious tone.

Mrs. Loudon replies that he does.

"Well, it's really extraordinary to me how he knows which road to take. All these roads look just the same to me — mountains on one side or the other, or in front or behind, and forests scattered about! If *I* had to drive we should probably go round in circles, and end up at Burnside in time for tea. Imagine Mary's feelings if we walked in at tea-time after all the trouble she's had cutting the sandwiches and filling the thermoses. By the way, I often wonder if it is correct to say thermoses for the plural. Dear Papa was very particular about grammar. There were no thermoses in those days, of course, but I remember how he jumped on me for talking about crocuses — or it may have been irises. I can't remember what the right way is, which shows it did not do me much good, doesn't it?

"Dear me, what a dangerous place!" she continues, as we skirt a precipice at the bottom of which a small blue loch lies dreaming in the afternoon sunshine. "If Dobbie were to take his hands off the wheel for an instant we should shoot over the edge, and nobody any the wiser. You may smile, Elspeth, but look at the dreadful accidents you read of in the papers. Who knows but Dobbie might take it into his head to put an end to us all, and nobody to know it wasn't an accident? People *do* get queer ideas like that sometimes. It was only this morning I read in the papers about a man who shot his wife and three children, because they could not agree where to go for their holidays — only it turned out afterwards that the woman was not *really* his *wife*, which, of course, makes a difference."

Mrs. Loudon usually bears Mrs. Falconer's wanderings with remarkable patience, but she has evidently reached the end of her tether. Quite suddenly she rouses herself, and remarks irritably, "Do you mean that Dobbie is likely to murder us all because he is not married to me?"

"*Married to you? Dobbie?* — my dear Elspeth, I am sure the man has never *thought* of it," says Mrs. Falconer, aghast.

"I could suggest it to him, of course," replies Mrs. Loudon reflectively.

"Elspeth, you can't be serious! *What* put such an extraordinary idea into your head?"

"You did, Millie."

"I?" gasps poor Mrs. Falconer.

"You seemed to think we should all be safer if I were married to Dobbie."

"Elspeth, you misunderstood me *entirely* —"

At this moment we fortunately arrive at our destination, and the subject is dropped. Tony Morley is waiting for us. "The others have gone on," he says. "Young Betty decided to go with them — she is one of those fortunate people who never know when they are *de trop*. Young Betty is in great form to-day. Give me that basket and the rug, Hester."

Through the trees I can see glimpses of green water. We follow Tony down a narrow path, and presently find ourselves standing in the shadow of a towering mass of rock. A toy castle is perched securely on the top, its windows gape with sightless eyes, and, here and there, a piece of crumbled wall or a roofless tower shows that it is no longer habitable. The whole thing is so battered by the weather, and so welded with the natural rock, that it is impossible to tell where the one ends and the other begins. Down the dark smooth sides of the cliff there trickles a constant film of water, and in every crevice grow moss and feathery ferns.

"What an impregnable fortress!" I whisper to Tony — there is an eerie silence in the place which one fears to break.

"Shall we climb the rock?" he suggests. "It is fairly steep, but there is a wonderful view from the top."

I agree, and we set off up a steep stony path which leads us — after a breath-taking climb — into the courtyard of the castle. This is paved with solid rock and is open to the sky. There is a well in the centre. Only one of the towers remains in reasonable repair. It contains a stone stairway worn by countless feet, and a small round room which actually boasts a roof.

The view from the window of the tower is indeed marvellous. The loch stretches in both directions. It is a peculiar shade of green, and is surrounded on all sides by tall trees which, in some places, lean over the water. There is something rather uncanny about the place; perhaps this feeling of something uncanny and awesome exists only in my own imagination — which was so stirred by the tale of Hector and Seónaid — perhaps not. I can well believe that this loch is not like other lochs.

Tony points out Seónaid's Bay — a little cove of white sand about two hundred yards from the Castle. It was here that her body was discovered by the women going down to wash their clothes.

We visit the dungeon — a damp, dark cave in the solid rock — and peer through the rusting bars into the green water below us, as many a poor creature must have done long ago. "I don't suppose the MacArbins kept their prisoners here very long," says Tony comfortingly. "It was so easy to get rid of them on account of the peculiarity of the loch. Just one little push, and away they went, never to be seen again —"

I ask Tony if he thinks the Castle is very old.

"It was built sometime in the thirteenth century by one Dermid MacArbin," Tony replies. "The clan was here before that, of course, but just living in hovels or caves in the mountains. This Dermid was the second son, and therefore of little importance in the scheme of things, but, being of an ambitious turn of mind, he killed his elder brother, and threw his body into the loch, thereby becoming head of the clan. Dermid's first act as chief was to set about the building of a stronghold — Castle Darroch. Some say he imported an Italian architect, others that he designed the place himself; in any case it is a very creditable piece of work, considering the primitive tools at his command. Every stone had to be hewn out of the solid rock, and carried up the cliff by human labour — of course, the whole clan toiled at it, and, I expect, they cursed old Dermid properly when his back was turned. Dermid must have been very proud of the Castle — it must have been exciting watching it grow, day by day, and seeing his dream take shape — but he never lived to enjoy it, for the very day that it was finished his brother's ghost rose up out of the loch and carried him off."

The scene is so awe-inspiring that the story is easily believed — those dark green waters look as though they could hold many a fearsome secret.

"But Dermid's dream-fortress remained," I suggest thoughtfully.

"Yes, it was the MacArbin stronghold for many centuries, until civilisation taught them to value comfort higher than safety," replies Tony, who seems to have the history of the place by heart. "The present MacArbin's grandfather built a hideous square house farther down the loch and allowed the castle to fall into ruins. Perhaps he felt slightly unsafe in the new house after his fortress, for he surrounded it with a palisade of high iron railings, so that it looks for all the world like a lion in a cage at the Zoo. There are no ghosts there, but their absence is made up for by three bathrooms, complete with hot and cold. My informant was the waiter at the Hotel; he is keeping company with Miss MacArbin's housemaid, so, of course, he knows all there is to know about them."

"What a pity!" I exclaim.

"Good heavens, would you rather have ghosts than bathrooms, Hester?" cries Tony in amazement. "You are incurably romantic! Or do you mean that you would like to see the MacArbins living in their stronghold with their ghosts, but not to live here yourself? If so, I agree with you, people should not think of their own comfort;

101

they should continue to live in their ancestral halls to add to the interest of the countryside.

"Let us people these ruins with long-dead MacArbins. There was the one who threw herself into the loch because her lover was killed at Culloden Moor, and another who was drowned in the loch in a sudden storm beneath the very walls of his home and in full view of his wife and children. His wife pined away and was dead in a month, so they threw her body into the loch to keep him company. I will show you the stone commemorating their fate as we go back — and then there was Seónaid, of course —"

"Were there no happy ones?" I ask sadly.

"Look at the surroundings," he replies. "Nobody could be *happy* here. The stage is set for tragedy. One could imagine wild scenes of excitement, and orgies of feasting and banqueting, but there could never be peace and happiness amongst scenery like this."

We climb the slimy stair and emerge once more into the courtyard. It is very still, and the sun shines down, painting strong shadows across the stones.

"Who's that?" says Tony suddenly in a queer voice.

I look up in time to see a tall woman, all in white, disappear into the doorway of the little tower.

"I suppose it was Elsie Baker," he adds in a not very convincing tone of voice.

"It was much too tall," I reply breathlessly. "And Elsie has a bright green frock on — who could it have been?"

"Somebody playing jokes, I suppose," says Tony. "I'll go and see who it is. Wait here for me, Hester."

I sit down on a corner of the ruined rampart to wait for him. Far down below, like toy figures on the green grass, I can see Mrs. Loudon and Mrs. Falconer laying the cloth for tea. It is strange to see everything so quiet and to remember the wild scenes this place has witnessed. How many times have these old walls echoed and re-echoed with the wild cries of battle when the MacQuills attacked their hereditary foes! From this eyrie the fierce Hector stole his bride, and here, within this very building, she revenged his death and met her own. These walls have sheltered joys, and sorrows, and hopes and fears innumerable; they have rung with the noise of revelry and the sound of grief; children have been born, and grown to manhood and died within their shelter — and now they are crumbling to ruin, fit only for the owl and the jackdaw to live in and build their nests.

It would not be strange if the place were haunted, visited by some of the fierce creatures who have dwelt here, and suffered, and known it as their home.

Thus musing I pass the time until I see Tony returning from his quest.

"There's nobody," he says with a laugh. "It must have been the effect of light on the wall."

"Nonsense, Tony," I reply sharply. "It was a woman dressed in white; she must have gone out some other way."

"She must have had wings, then," says Tony. "I've looked everywhere, and there's no other way out of the tower."

"But I *saw* her."

103

"Well, I suppose she flew out of the window, then," he replies rather crossly.

"*You* saw her first," I point out.

"I thought I did, but now I know I didn't," he retorts.

We wrangle half-heartedly about the disappearing lady as we climb down the steep path to tea.

By this time the rugs have been spread out and the tea laid beneath the spreading branches of a great oak. I am relieved to hear my daughter's voice, and to see her appear with Guthrie and Elsie from among the trees. This place has a disquieting effect upon my nerves; it is the sort of place where anything horrible might happen.

Betty comes running up to us, calling out that Guthrie found an owl's nest in a big tree and there was a little owl in it all soft and furry. The others say nothing about their adventures, but take their places in silence, Guthrie sitting down between me and Tony, and leaving Miss Baker to find a place for herself.

"I say, Loudon, you're sitting on a thistle," says Tony with solicitude. "Wouldn't you be more comfortable on the rug?"

"I am quite comfortable where I am," Guthrie replies ungraciously.

"I wouldn't like to sit on a thistle," gurgles Betty, between two mouthfuls of egg sandwich.

Apart from this slightly acrimonious exchange, tea is a silent meal. Mrs. Falconer is in one of her silent moods, and confines her remarks to requests for more tea or another scone. Elsie and Guthrie are obviously out of tune, and my thoughts are busy with the phenomenon of the lady in white.

The place itself is sufficient to depress the spirits of most people. There is a damp chill feeling in the air, for the sunshine never falls on this side of the rock. The trees are covered with moss and lichen, and a few bright red toadstools cluster round their roots. A huge black bird flies past slowly, the flap of its wings echoing strangely from the overhanging cliff.

"Raven," says Tony quietly.

Just at this moment there is a loud peal of thunder, and a gust of wind steals through the trees, shaking their heavy branches and stirring the green water on the loch.

"We had better get back to the cars," Mrs. Loudon says, looking anxiously at the sky, which has clouded over with remarkable suddenness. "It's going to rain, and when it rains here it comes down in buckets."

"Oh no, don't let's go!" cries Betty. "It's lovely — just like the pantomime before the wizard appears. It gives me the same shuddery feeling in my spine."

"There's MacQuill," says Guthrie suddenly, looking up from his task of packing the basket of crockery. "Shall I shout to him to come with us? He'll get drenched."

We all look up, and I am just in time to see a man running up the little path between the trees. He is wearing a grey flannel suit and has no hat.

"It can't be Hector MacQuill," Tony points out. "This is the last place *he* would come."

"It *was* Hector. I saw him distinctly," replies Guthrie, white with rage.

Tony merely smiles incredulously.

I realise there are the makings of a first-class row — it seems strange that these two men can never speak to each other without getting hot.

"Whoever it was, he will get frightfully wet," I remark pacifically, as a few large splashes of rain fall on my bare arms, and another peal of thunder echoes rumblingly amongst the mountains.

"It was Hector MacQuill," says Guthrie obstinately. He picks up two large baskets and several rugs, and, thus laden, marches off.

The rest of us collect the remainder of the feast, and follow him as fast as we are able. Dobbie is struggling with the hood of the Bentley. Tony rushes to help him. We all scramble into our seats, and the coats and rugs are thrown in on the top of us. Then the heavens seem to open, and the rain comes down in a blinding white sheet of water. The very trees bend under its weight.

"It's not been a very nice afternoon," Dobbie remarks, understating the facts with typical Lowland phlegm, as he climbs into his seat and shuts the door. I notice that, in these few moments, his uniform is soaked through, and the water is trickling down the back of his neck.

Mrs. Loudon agrees with him; she is too used to Dobbie's imperturbability to be surprised at his words.

"Will we start home, Mrs. Loudon?" he enquires, mopping his face with a blue handkerchief, "or will we wait a wee while till the shower's past?"

The "shower" is drumming on the roof like the rattle of musketry, and Mrs. Loudon has to raise her voice to make herself heard.

"We'll get home as quickly as we can," she says. "I'll not have your death at my door, sitting there dripping as if you'd just been taken out of the loch. Away home, and mind you get changed as soon as possible."

Dobbie murmurs something about "a wee thing damp," but he knows Mrs. Loudon too well to argue about it, and soon we are squelching through the mud like a buffalo in a wallow, with the rain beating on the windows and the thunder growling overhead.

"Who would have thought it would turn out like this?" enquires Mrs. Falconer blandly. "It reminds me of a picnic I went to when I was a child —"

The thunder has made my head ache, so I lie back in my corner and try not to hear; but it is impossible not to hear. Why are we not provided with ear-lids to work in the same way as eyelids, so that if we want to be quiet we may shut our ears and drift away upon our own thoughts? As it is I am forced to listen to a lengthy account of the picnic which Mrs. Falconer attended at the age of eight, clad in a muslin frock and a blue sash. To-day being what it is, and Mrs. Falconer being reminded of the occasion by the storm, it is only logical to suppose that these frail garments were completely ruined by the elements; but I can't be certain of this, for I never heard the story finished. Mrs. Loudon, who for some time has been wrapped in her own thoughts — perhaps *she* has invisible ear lids — suddenly leans forward and says:

"Dobbie — was that young Mr. MacQuill who passed up the path just before the storm broke?"

"There wasn't anybody passed *me*," Dobbie replies. "I never saw anybody all the time I was there. It's a lonely sort of spot — a bit eerie to my mind."

"Yes, it is," replies Mrs. Loudon thoughtfully.

I can see she is puzzled by the mystery of the disappearing man (and it certainly seems very queer, for the path he took was narrow and led only to the place where we left the cars) but the disappearing lady was an even more perplexing phenomenon, and I can't help wondering what Mrs. Loudon would have made of that. For myself I can make nothing of it at all, and, in spite of an inner voice which assures me that there are no such things as ghosts, I am forced to the somewhat awesome conclusion that there must be, and that I have seen one with my own eyes in broad daylight. If Tony had not seen it too — but then he did. It is all very puzzling.

THURSDAY: 9TH JUNE

GUTHRIE IS DISILLUSIONED

Guthrie says, "But people *do* take the wrong turning sometimes, Hester, and then they can't go back."

We have been talking trivialities until now — I can't remember what — but there is suddenly a strained note in Guthrie's voice which catches my attention and holds it fast. I roll over on the soft turf and look at him in surprise. He is raised on one elbow, and is very busy digging little holes in the grass with his fingers.

High up in the blue sky a lark is singing a perfect pæan of praise to its Creator, the loch dreams in the sunshine, devoid of the slightest ripple, a faint haze hovers over the low marshy ground, and shimmers in the noonday heat.

"But people can always go back to the cross-roads, Guthrie."

"Not in life," he says gravely.

Suddenly my heart hammers in my throat, and I search wildly for words. "Guthrie, if people have only gone a little way down the wrong road, they can still turn back — the cross-roads are in sight —"

"No," he replies, digging his little holes with frightful industry. "No, Hester. A man's got to go forward all the time. Besides, people are sometimes farther down the road than you think — distance is deceptive sometimes."

"Guthrie!"

"Let's go home," he says. "It's hopeless for fishing to-day. I think I shall take my gun, and get a few rabbits for Mother."

As we stroll over the hill I search wildly for words to influence Guthrie. Quite obviously his strange talk refers to his relations with Elsie. He has come to see her in her true light, but intends — like the obstinate chivalrous creature he is — to marry her all the same. It would have been bad enough for him to marry Elsie thinking her a paragon amongst women, but to marry her with no such delusion is infinitely worse. Sailors don't see very much of their wives, and Guthrie might have gone on for years thinking her perfect in every way. The awful thing about it is that it is all my fault. I have laid myself out to be nice to him. I have tried to show him that a woman can be a friend, and it seems that he has learnt his lesson only too well. I have rushed in where angels might well have feared to tread, and destroyed his illusions to no purpose. Far better if I had left Guthrie alone, and returned to Biddington by the first train. Far better if I had stood aside, or made myself deliberately disagreeable to the man. This is what comes of trying to meddle with people's lives; you achieve your object and find it is a disaster.

At last I can bear it no longer, and I seize my companion by the arm.

"Guthrie!" I cry, "it's not fair to tell me a little and then not let me speak to you. You've simply got to listen to me."

He smiles down at me a little wearily. "My dear, I didn't mean to tell you anything. I'm kicking myself now — if that's any consolation to you."

"None whatever," I reply firmly. "Sit down there and let me speak to you."

We sit down upon a fallen tree, whereupon speech deserts me. I have so much to say that nothing will come.

"Well, go on," he says quite gently.

"Guthrie, you really mustn't do it," I say at last. "You've no idea what you're doing, or you would not *think* of it. You've no idea what marriage is. I've been married for twelve years, and I can tell you this — happiness is only possible when two people have the same ideas."

"Everybody says marriage is a lottery, so what does it matter?" says Guthrie.

"It may be a lottery, but why draw the wrong number on purpose?" I reply quickly.

"I've drawn my number."

"Oh, Guthrie, do listen to me! Don't make a mess of your whole life because you are too proud to say you have made a mistake."

"There is no question of making a mess of my life. Elsie is a dear little girl, and I'm very fond of her; it is only —"

"It is only that you have nothing in common," I interrupt him breathlessly. "Guthrie, do listen to me,

111

and believe that I know what I'm talking about — it wouldn't be quite so bad if you could marry and settle down in a home with friends round you, and each have your own interests and amusements, but Service people can't do that. They've *got* to be pals, making each other do for everything, finding their home, and their friends, and their interests all in each other."

He looks at me with a face gone suddenly white under its tan. "My dear, I know. But I can't go back — she trusts me — she has promised to marry me."

I cry to him angrily, "And do you suppose that *she* will be happy? Be sensible for *her* sake if you won't be sensible for your own."

"I think I can make her happy," he replies stiffly.

We walk on in silence.

FRIDAY: 10TH JUNE

BETTY GOES FISHING — THE DINNER-PARTY

Mrs. Loudon announces at breakfast that she is going to have a dinner-party. The announcement is received by Guthrie with unmitigated scorn. He says that dinner-parties are a winter sport, only just bearable in towns where people are herded together in any case — and that it will spoil an evening's fishing, and, anyway, nobody will come.

Mrs. Loudon replies with spirit that *he* need not come unless he wants to, there are plenty of people to ask. That nice Major Morley, for instance.

Guthrie says *he* won't come.

Mrs. Loudon retorts that we shall see whether he will or not, but, for her part, she has no doubt about it — and we can ask Miss Baker and her father, if Guthrie likes.

Guthrie says *he* won't come, *anyway* — he never goes out anywhere.

Mrs. Loudon says if he doesn't want to come he can refuse the invitation, and she intends to ask the MacArbins, because they never have any fun, and Hester ought to see them.

Guthrie says why not ask the MacQuills too.

Mrs. Loudon says it's a pity we can't, but it might be a little *too* exciting if they went for each other in the drawing-room.

Guthrie says, "My God, what a party!" and opens the newspaper ostentatiously.

Mrs. Loudon repairs to her desk, writes three notes in record time, and summons Dobbie to deliver them — she is not in the habit of letting the grass grow under her feet.

"— and we can just go ahead with the preparations," she says, looking at me over the top of her spectacles as she sits at her desk. "For they'll all jump at it."

"When is it to be?" I ask her.

"To-night, of course," replies the indomitable woman. "Where's the sense of putting things off? If I'm feeling like having a dinner-party, I have it. And you can dress the flowers for the table," she adds trenchantly, "for I know perfectly well that you'll not let *me* do it in peace."

I am about to leave the room when Mrs. Loudon recalls me — "Salmon, and lamb, and peas, and trifle," she says, frowning anxiously. "Would you give them soup as well, Hester, or yon new-fangled grape-fruit?"

I vote for soup, whereupon Mrs. Loudon's brow clears.

"It's cold fare for an empty stomach, grape-fruit," she says. "I'll admit they always give me the goose-flesh. Whereas a nice spoonful of *Julienne* is a comforting sort of start."

114

Guthrie now appears, looking quite pleasant again —
his ill humours are always short-lived — and remarks
that there is a fine breeze on the loch, and can Hester
come, or does his mother intend to work her all day
long like a galley-slave over this forsaken dinner?

Mrs. Loudon replies that *she* does not work Hester
like a galley-slave, and perhaps Guthrie has forgotten
that galley-slaves were used to row ships when he chose
that particular metaphor.

Guthrie actually has the grace to blush, though
protesting, not altogether truthfully, that we always take
it in turns to row.

We collect the fishing tackle and make our way down
to the loch, where we find Betty and a boy of about her
own age — or slightly older — digging in the gravel.
Annie is sitting close by, knitting a multi-coloured
jumper, which, I feel sure, must be intended for
Bollings — Tim's batman — to whom she is engaged.

Guthrie says he has no idea who the boy can be
unless he is one of Donald's offspring, which are
numbered as the sands of the sea. I reply that Betty
would find another child to play with her if she were
marooned upon a desert island.

At this moment Betty sees us, and calls out that Ian
is showing her how to dam the burn with stones.
Guthrie says *he* knows how to damn the burn without
stones.

"Oh, do you? *How?*" says Betty with interest.

I feel slightly worried at the probable development of
this conversation, as it looks as though it might turn out

115

to have a damaging effect upon my child's morals (no pun intended).

Ian now remarks, in a soft Highland voice, that he is aware the burn *could* be dammed with sods, but he doots the laird would not like us to be cutting them.

I can see that Guthrie is about to say that he can damn it without sods, so I make a face at him and he remains silent.

Betty now says that she is tired of damming burns, so can she and Ian come fishing with us if they promise to be very quiet? (She knows from experience that this promise usually appeals to the adult mind.) Guthrie says they may, and we all embark without further ado.

It is a grey, cloudy day with small ripples and a whitish glare upon the water. The top of Ben Seoch is swathed in mist. Guthrie takes out his rod and says solemnly he is doubtful about the fish to-day. They don't as a rule take well with mist on the mountains. I reply facetiously that the fish can't possibly know about the mist unless somebody has told them.

"But the kelpies tell them, of course," replies Guthrie gravely. "I thought you knew that much, Hester. How ignorant you are, to be sure!"

Ian gazes at Guthrie with large brown eyes, and asks if Mr. Loudon has ever seen a kelpie talking to the fishes. This puts the good man in rather a hole, and he spends some time fabricating a long and somewhat complicated answer to the question.

After a couple of drifts during which no rise is seen, Betty begins to get slightly restive, and asks why Guthrie doesn't catch a fish — don't the fish *want* to

116

get caught? *She* thinks that fish like worms best, and, if Guthrie likes, she and Ian will go and dig some up for him. Bryan always uses worms when he goes fishing.

Ian suddenly says, "Whisht" and points to a ring in the water about twenty yards from the boat. He is obviously no tyro at the sport. We approach our prey, and Guthrie casts over the place with great skill. A large fish rises and looks at the flies disdainfully, but utterly refuses to be caught. Betty reiterates her conviction that fish prefer worms.

The morning passes without success. We learn from Ian that he is indeed the son of Donald, and that he intends to become a ghillie. Guthrie suggests the Navy as a more suitable profession, but Ian is not attracted by the idea and says he would not like to be spending his whole time climbing masts; it would be an easier thing to be tracking the deer upon the mountains — so it would.

After some time spent in flogging the water without any result, even Guthrie has to admit that it seems pretty useless, and we return home with an empty bag. We are walking back to the house somewhat disconsolately, when Betty suddenly turns to me and asks with her usual directness, "What is the *use* of fishing, Mummie?"

I am slightly taken aback, but reply, after a moment's thought, that it is to catch fish, of course.

"I'm sure I could invent a better way," she says. "I would make a little trap for them with flies inside — if they really *like* flies, though *I* think they like worms better — and then, when they were all inside eating the

117

flies — or worms — the trapdoor would shut, and there they'd be."

Guthrie says bitterly that after this morning's so-called sport he is inclined to agree with Betty.

Betty says, after reflection, that she likes damming burns much better than fishing.

The afternoon is spent doing the flowers — a task which is made more difficult for me by Mrs. Loudon, whose ideas on floral decorations have already been chronicled. We also write out the *menu* cards, and arrange how everyone is to sit at table.

"I wonder what like that Baker man will be?" says Mrs. Loudon. "I'll have to have him on my left, and I'll put you next to him, so mind and talk to the creature, Hester, and you can have Major Morley on the other side to make up."

"What good will that be if I can't talk to him?" I enquire innocently.

"You know what I mean well enough," she replies. "You're getting too uppish altogether, and if there's any more of it I'll pack you off home. Now where will we put Miss MacArbin?"

Our deliberations are interrupted by the arrival of the post, and I am overjoyed to receive a letter from Tim. He has written before, of course, but only miserable, scrappy communications to convey the news that he is well and very busy getting his company into trim. This letter looks more promising, and I have hopes that it may contain information about houses. Perhaps Tim has had time to visit some of the "desirable residences to let" whose names I obtained from the agent at Biddington.

"Away with you and read it in peace," Mrs. Loudon says suddenly, so I fly upstairs with it to digest it at my leisure.

The letter begins with the announcement that Tim has been very busy with his company, but that he has found time to examine some of the pigsties on the agent's list, and most of them are absolutely foul. There is only one he likes the look of — it is called "Heathery Hill," on account of one small piece of heather which is dragging out an exiled existence in the rockery. I perceive at once that the charm of "Heathery Hill" consists in the fact that there is a stable at the back which Tim can use for his charger, and I have grave doubts whether Tim has looked at any of its other amenities. The beds, the furniture, the kitchen range, and water supply, the condition of the roof, and the drains are completely ignored in Tim's description. He touches lightly on the fact that the drawing-room has a southern aspect, and the existence of a cupboard under the stairs, and asks me to wire at once whether or not he is to take it, as there are several other people after it. This threat does not disturb me, as agents invariably try to hustle prospective tenants in this manner, but I hastily scan the remainder of Tim's letter in the hope that I may gather a few more crumbs of information anent my future home. Alas, there are no more crumbs! The rest of the letter deals exclusively with a description of his charger, whom he has named Boanerges on account of his dark colour and rolling

119

eye. Tim hopes that I approve of the name. Boanerges is absolutely the pick of the officers' mounts, but not up to the Colonel's weight, of course, and old MacPherson likes something quieter. He is very comfortable to ride, and has excellent paces. Boanerges seems such an admirable steed that I can't help wondering why he has been relegated to the junior major of the Battalion — perhaps the postscript explains in some part the anomaly; it is added in pencil and is ominously brief — "Have just discovered, rather unexpectedly, that Boanerges does not like his father."

I dress early for the dinner-party, and don my new frock with great satisfaction. It is beige lace with orange flowers, and I note in the mirror that it is really very becoming.

Betty calls to me to come and say "Good night" to her, and, when I comply with her request, I find her having her supper in bed, with the faithful Annie in attendance.

"Oh, you *do* look nice, m'm!" exclaims the latter ecstatically.

Betty looks at me appraisingly, and says that *she* likes me much better in my Fair Isle jumper.

"But your mother could never wear it for dinner," says the scandalised Annie.

"Why not?" asks Betty truculently. "When I'm grown up I shall wear what I like best all the time — I shall wear my pyjamas all day if I want to."

I kiss my daughter, and suggest to Annie in an undertone that perhaps a little fig syrup might be a good thing, and, having fulfilled my maternal duties, wend my way downstairs.

Although I am early on the scene my hostess is before me. She is seated by the fire, looking very dignified in black lace, and engaged in reading *The Times*, which only reaches this remote spot at dinner-time.

She looks up and says, "I hoped you'd be early. What a pretty thing you are! Come and warm yourself, child."

I sit down beside her chair on a footstool, and we both gaze at the fire for a little while without speaking. A fire of birch logs is a lovely sight. The under part glows redly, like a miniature forge, and little blue tongues of flame come licking round the bark as if it tastes nice.

At last Mrs. Loudon breaks the spell of silence. "Hester, I'm beginning to think Guthrie sees through that girl," she says thoughtfully. "What do you think about it?"

I don't know what to reply — I would tell her about our conversation if I thought she could persuade Guthrie where I have failed, but she couldn't, I know. If she were to speak to him they would both lose their tempers, and there would be a row, and Guthrie would rush off and marry the girl offhand. Besides, if he *is* going to marry the girl it will be better for Mrs. Loudon to think that he is still infatuated with her. All these thoughts have boiled in my head for two days, until I am quite muddled with them. I see no loop-hole of escape. Guthrie has all his mother's obstinacy in him —

he is determined to marry Elsie — and the more opposition he finds to his foolish course, the more determined he will be.

"Well?" she says. "You haven't answered — what a girl you are for dreaming!" She turns my face up to hers and looks at me earnestly. "He has spoken to you," she says, in a breathless voice.

"He is quite determined to marry her," I reply in the same low tone. "My dear, you will have to make the best of it. I've done all I can. I'm sorry."

Mrs. Loudon clings to my hand. "He's all I've got left," she says, "and I can't be friends with that girl. She's got nothing in her that I can get hold of — nothing that I can understand. She's not a bad girl, I know, but she's just different. She'll take Guthrie right away from me — she hates me."

"She's rather frightened of you, I think."

"Yes, I suppose I *am* rather a fearsome old woman to people — to people who don't understand my way," she says pathetically. "It's the way I'm made, and I'm too old to change now."

I hold her tightly. I can hear her heart beating very quickly under my ear, and feel the rise and fall of her hurried breathing.

"It will ruin him," she says, still in that low breathless voice. "They will both be miserable. He needs a woman to understand him — for the creature's a fool in some ways, though I say it. The right woman could have made Guthrie, the wrong woman will ruin him."

Of course she is right. I can only hold her thin body close and pat her shoulder.

"Gracious me!" she exclaims at last, pushing me away and blowing her nose loudly on a large linen handkerchief. "What a fool I am! It's no wonder Guthrie's one, with a mother like me. Here are we, croaking like sybils, and guests expected any minute! Me with a red nose, too! No, Hester, you can keep your powder — I'm too old now to start powdering my nose. If it's red, it's red, and there's an end to it."

"It's not very red," I reassure her.

"That's a mercy," she replies. "For they'll be here directly. Dobbie's gone to fetch the MacArbins. They're very poor, and their car is a ramshackle affair to go out at night. By the way, Guthrie said I was to warn you that you've to call the man MacArbin — they're a brother and sister, you know — 'last scions of a noble race.'"

"Mr. MacArbin," I suggest, wondering what else I would be likely to call him.

"No, just MacArbin — here they are, I declare — he's *the* MacArbin, you see."

I don't see, and decide not to address the man under any circumstances whatever, and then I shall not betray my ignorance.

His appearance completely overwhelms me. I have seen lots of kilts, but never one worn with such an air of confidence and pride.

"Mrs. Christie, may I introduce MacArbin," says my hostess, in her dignified manner.

We both bow, he with a strangely foreign grace, which seems to spread upwards from the chased silver buckles on his shoes to the crown of his iron-grey hair.

I take in at a glance the perfection of his attire: his green kilt, his snowy falls of lace at neck and wrist, the silver buttons on his black cloth doublet, the jewelled dagger in his stocking. From this I go on to take stock of himself: flashing brown eyes, long thin nose, long thin fingers and sensitive hands — and decide that here, indeed, is the portrait of a Highland gentleman come to life.

I try to think of some remark — not too utterly inane — to address him with, but can think of nothing more original than the weather. We decide that it was fine this morning, but somewhat showery in the afternoon, and then look at each other blankly.

Fortunately Tony Morley arrives to rescue me, and the two men are soon deep in the technicalities of stalking. I am thus able to observe them at my leisure. They are typical examples of their race. Tony's tail-coat makes him look taller, while the Highlander's kilt gives him breadth with grace. It suits me well that they should talk to each other, for I want to be at hand to help Mrs. Loudon if required.

Mrs. Falconer has captured Miss MacArbin, a tall slim girl in a night-blue frock, and is telling her a long and complicated story in confidential tones. I look with interest at Miss MacArbin and wonder whether Miss Campbell was correct in her surmise. I can easily understand any man falling madly in love with her, for there is something fatally attractive about her pale beauty and her rather languid grace.

Mrs. Loudon seizes my arm, and says: "Hester, I should never have asked the Bakers."

I realise the truth of this, but it is much too late now; in fact the Bakers' wheels are crunching over the gravel at this very moment. Guthrie goes into the hall to meet them, and returns escorting a small red-faced man with silver hair and amazingly bushy silver eyebrows. He shakes hands all round, and says, with a beaming smile, that he is pleased to meet us — he is really rather a lovable little man.

"I'm so glad you could come," Mrs. Loudon says. "Your daughter told us you don't go out much."

"Oh well, it's not everybody wants the old man," replies Mr. Baker with engaging simplicity. "But I just said to Elsie — I *must* go to Mrs. Loudon's party, seeing she's been good enough to ask me. Elsie wasn't too keen on me coming, but you must be firm sometimes, and, after all, you've *got* to see me sooner or later. Of course it's quite natural Elsie shouldn't want to have me tagged on to her — my little girl can take her place in any society — I tell you I'm proud of my little Elsie, she's all I've got, ma'am. I've spared no expense to give her a good education, and I tell you I've got my money's worth."

There is an awkward pause in the general conversation. I, for one, am speechless, and the others seem to be in a like condition. Mrs. Falconer finds her tongue first, and dashes into the breach — is it sheer good luck, or is she not really quite so vague and foolish as she seems?

"That is just what dear Papa always said," she announces ecstatically. "'A good education is the best foundation,' he used to say. I've always remembered it

125

because it rhymes — and it's so *true*, isn't it? I always think it is easier to remember things when they rhyme. We used to learn history like that:

> " 'Ten sixty-six on Hastings' strand
> Harold the Norman comes to land.' "

Guthrie has now started to hand round sherry. I have just taken a glass from the tray when I look up and see Elsie Baker standing at the door, her eyes fixed upon MacArbin with an incredulous stare. She is obviously on the brink of hysterical laughter. This would be fatal, so I edge nearer to her and whisper:

"Isn't he magnificent, Miss Baker? *The* MacArbin, you know. Descended from the great chief —"

"My!" she exclaims with a gasp. "He's just like Duggie Fairweather in *Scotland's Bath of Blood*."

I realise at once, with relief, that she has no higher meed of praise, and drink my sherry in peace.

Everyone is now talking at the top of his voice — an excellent sign at this stage of the proceedings. We finish our sherry, and are herded into the dining-room, and distributed round the table by our hostess.

MacArbin sits upon his hostess's right, then comes Mrs. Falconer and Elsie Baker. Guthrie and Miss MacArbin are next, and then Tony and myself, with Mr. Baker on Mrs. Loudon's left.

Tony starts his nonsense before we have finished the excellent *Julienne*, and I realise that he is in one of his most irresponsible moods.

126

"Is this a betrothal feast?" he whispers. "The gloom upon the brow of our good hostess is more fitting to the baked meats of a funeral collation."

"You will probably get an excellent dinner," I reply shortly.

"I don't doubt it," says Tony, "but it is most essential for me to know whether I am to be my usual gay and witty self — the life and soul of the party — or to put on the gloomy gravity which I invariably reserve for sad and solemn occasions."

I reply that he can do as he pleases, and turn my left shoulder towards him — he really deserves a snub. Unfortunately Mr. Baker is too deep in conversation with Mrs. Loudon to notice my movement, and I have the choice of listening to the said conversation — which I realise is of a distinctly private nature — or withdrawing my left shoulder from Tony and making it up with him.

"It's a good little business," Mr. Baker is saying earnestly. "Two thousand a year it brings in, regular as clockwork — too much for a man with simple tastes like me. Elsie likes her comforts, you know, and I shall settle a thousand a year on her if she marries the right chap — or I'd be willing to take him into the business and expand a bit."

Mrs. Loudon says she is delighted to hear he is so comfortably off, but implies delicately that she is not interested in his financial affairs.

"Oh, I dare say I'm a bit premature, as the chicken said when it cracked the shell," replies Mr. Baker, winking at her slyly. "But I do like to have things cut

127

and dried and above-board. You're quite right to pull me up a bit, ma'am. Elsie said herself I was to go easy, and I'll go as easy as you please. You'll drive me on a snaffle before we've gone far, see if you don't."

Mrs. Loudon's face is a study; she gazes at Mr. Baker as if he were some strange and rather dangerous reptile, but she is too rigid in her ideas of hospitality to attempt a snub. Besides, the little man is so devoid of all desire to offend, his friendliness and simplicity are disarming. Her eyes meet mine with a pleading, anguished look. "Hester, I don't know if I introduced Mr. Baker," she murmurs weakly.

"Indeed you did, ma'am; you know your job as hostess, as anyone can see with half an eye," replies Mr. Baker gallantly. "You introduced Mrs. Christie and me right off, and very pleased I was. I've heard a lot about Mrs. Christie from some friends of hers staying at the Hotel — Mr. and Mrs. MacTurk."

I try to explain that I don't know them very well, but Mr. Baker does not listen. "Very nice friends to have, Mrs. Christie, especially the lady. She's always saying how sorry she is at you leaving Kiltwinkle. It must be a bit trying for a lady like you not to have a settled home of your own, isn't it now?"

This statement is often made to me, and it always annoys me, chiefly, I think, because it is true. But some time ago I found a quotation which seemed to meet the case, and I always make use of it on these occasions.

"'To a resolved mind his home is everywhere,'" I reply sententiously.

Mr. Baker looks suitably impressed, but Tony, who has now recovered from my snub, and has evidently been able to make very little of Miss MacArbin, turns round and says, "Since when have you had a resolved mind, O Dame of the Burning Pestle? The quotation is apt, I admit, and the provocation considerable, but I should advise you to keep your erudite literary quotations for an erudite literary audience. To cast pearls before swine is not a sign of superiority, but the sign of a narrow mind. Swine have their own standard of values, and a really clever and adaptable person should be able to adapt himself to his company."

"Grunt at them, I suppose," I suggest, for I am slightly hurt at being called narrow-minded.

Mr. Baker looks thoroughly puzzled at Tony's dissertation, but brightens up at the word "swine." "D'you know much about the value of swine, sir?" he asks interestedly. "I deal in 'ides, you know. Quite a paying business it is."

Mrs. Loudon has turned thankfully to the MacArbin, and is listening to his ideas on the subject of grouse moors with an appearance of intense interest.

Elsie now leans forward across the table and asks Tony if he was talking about *The Burning Thistle* — she thought she heard him mention it. She went to Inverness yesterday with a boy from the Hotel, and they saw it at the Picture House, and isn't Molly Greateyes just wonderful?

Tony replies, "Simply divine! That close-up in the second reel where the lovers are united after passing through fire and flood —"

Elsie knits her brows and says, "But that's not till the end of the fourth reel when they meet in the burning house."

"Oh, of course, the end of the *fourth* reel," agrees Tony. "And he seizes her in his arms and staggers out of the blazing pile, just when everyone thinks they are burned to death."

Elsie says she doesn't remember that bit, and I am not surprised to hear it, for, of course, Tony has never seen the film and is just being naughty.

Dinner flows on with admirable smoothness, for Mrs. Loudon's maids are well trained; but the conversation is interrupted by a good many cross-questions and crooked answers owing to the strange conglomeration of people which Mrs. Loudon has seen fit to invite. I find it difficult to converse with Tony and Mr. Baker at the same time. Their tastes are different and their outlook upon life irreconcilable, and can't help wishing that Mrs. Loudon would take part in entertaining my right-hand neighbour, or else that Miss MacArbin would produce some small talk for Tony.

Mrs. Falconer, who has been somewhat subdued, suddenly wakes up and starts telling the MacArbin about her old nurse who suffered greatly from chilblains. She even had one on her nose. Mrs. Falconer, who was then about seven years old, or possibly eight, made a little nose-bag and presented it to Old Nannie for a Christmas present. "The nose-bag was made of red flannel, and had two little pieces of elastic which went round the ears," continues Mrs. Falconer reminiscently. "I can see her now, going about her work with that little red bag on her nose. It really did her a lot of good — that, or the cod-liver oil which was ordered for her by the doctor. But one day she went to the back door in it by mistake, and the greengrocer's boy, who was handing in a bag of potatoes, nearly had a fit when he saw her, and poor Nannie was so offended at the way he laughed that she never wore the nose-bag again."

"— so there it is," Mr. Baker is saying with his beaming smile. "What do *you* think about it, Mrs. Christie?"

I gaze at him in despair, for I have not been listening to a word, and have no idea what I think about it. I have been caught out in the reprehensible act of listening to other people's conversation, and neglecting my own.

"It took me some time to get used to it," he admits with a chuckle. "But there, I'm only an old-fashioned buffer and girls have to be in the mode — and if Elsie's pleased, well, so am I!"

I smile at him vaguely.

"I see you haven't been done, Mrs. Christie," he whispers confidentially. "Elsie'd tell you where *she* went, in a minute she would. Very satisfied she was —"

What *is* the man talking about? Some sort of inoculation, perhaps.

"Are you going to be done?" I ask, hoping that his reply may elucidate the problem.

He looks at me and suddenly shouts with laughter. "Ha, ha! That's rich, that is. You're a wit, Mrs. Christie, and no mistake — ha, ha, ha. Fancy the old Dad having his eyebrows plucked! Ha, ha! Ha, ha, ha!"

The attention of the entire table is centred upon us. Mr. Baker mops his eyes with his table-napkin and then tries to stuff it into his pocket. "Ha, ha!" he shouts. "Ha, ha, ha! Thought it was my serviette — I mean my 'andkerchief — ha, ha, ha!"

The MacArbin places an eyeglass in his eye, and looks across the table at Mr. Baker as if he were a strange animal which has never been seen before. Guthrie asks what is the joke.

At this moment Mrs. Loudon gives the signal for departure — she evidently thinks it unsafe to wait until Mr. Baker recovers his breath. Mrs. Falconer, who has got behind-hand in dessert, owing to her story about old Nannie's nose-bag, is still eating an apple.

"Elspeth!" she exclaims piteously.

But Elspeth is already at the door, and Mrs. Falconer is obliged to clutch her pochette, and hasten after her fellow females.

"Elspeth is so unobservant," she whispers to me as we cross the hall. "And it was a Jonathan, too — my favourite kind."

In the drawing-room there is a moment's silence and then everybody speaks at once.

Elsie asks: "Whatever were you and Dad laughing at?"

Mrs. Falconer begins, "When us girls were all young —"

And Mrs. Loudon says, "Poke up the fire, Hester," and starts pushing chairs and sofas about with fierce and somewhat misplaced energy.

I poke up the fire, which incidentally requires no poking, and sit down beside Miss MacArbin. She looks dreamy and peaceful, and I am in need of peace. I feel slightly battered, and my face is stiff with smiling false smiles and hiding real ones.

"Castle Darroch is beautiful," I tell her. "We had a picnic there one day."

"But it is very sad," she says softly.

Miss MacArbin interests me in spite of her absence of small talk. Her beauty is almost startling. There is something timid, yet proud, in the carriage of her small, exquisitely shaped head, and her eyes are fiery and dreamy by turns. Why, of course, I tell myself suddenly, she is like a princess in a fairy-tale, and I feel glad to think I have found such an exact description of her.

"It is the atmosphere of Castle Darroch that is sad," she says, still in that soft silvery voice. "So many strange and terrible things have happened there —"

"I believe I saw a ghost," I tell her with a smile.

Miss MacArbin smiles too, and the smile lights up the wistfulness of her face like a sunbeam. "People often see ghosts when they *expect* to see them," she says lightly. "Perhaps you had read the story of Seónaid just before you went there. I used to play in the ruins when I was a child, but I never saw a ghost."

"This was a woman in white," I tell her. "She was rather like you — now I think of it — tall and slim with dark hair —"

133

She looks at me strangely. "I am supposed to be like Seónaid."

"Then you think it was the ghost of Seónaid we saw?"

"How can I tell you? I have never seen one."

She does not like the subject, for some reason — perhaps it is because she is superstitious and thinks it is unlucky to speak of ghosts. I look at her hands; they are very pretty, with long, tapering fingers — she has no engagement ring, so I conclude, reluctantly, that Miss Campbell was wrong in her surmise.

"I think you must have a very interesting life," she says suddenly, raising her eyes and looking at me with friendliness. "To move about the world as you do, and meet so many different people, must be very interesting."

"It has its disadvantages."

"Oh yes, but every kind of life has its disadvantages. You get so deeply in a groove if you go on living for ever and ever in the same place, and it is difficult to get out of a groove. It takes courage. I am rather frightened of people," she admits simply.

"People are really very nice."

"Yes," she says. "You would find them so, because you are not thinking of yourself all the time. I think of myself too much."

The advent of the men puts a stop to our conversation, and there is a general reshuffle of chairs. This is the worst of a dinner-party — or indeed any sort of party — you have no sooner begun to find out a little about your *vis-à-vis*, and become interested in her personality, than she is snatched away from you.

Mrs. Loudon suggests bridge, and the cards are produced by Guthrie. A great deal of discussion ensues as to who shall play and who shall sit out.

Tony comes over to where I am sitting and says, "It's lovely outside, Hester."

"Aren't you going to play?" I ask in surprise, for Tony Morley is known in the Regiment as an indomitable bridge player.

"There is a time and a place for everything," he replies gravely, "and this is neither the time nor the place for bridge."

We therefore go outside, and walk up and down the veranda once or twice, and then sit down in a comfortable friendly silence. If Guthrie were my companion he would want me to walk down to the gate and wreck my best shoes on the gravel, but Tony is never thoughtless in small matters.

It is lovely here, after the heat and chatter of the drawing-room — a few faint, rosy clouds linger above the mountains in a band of pale primrose sky, and a single faint star peeps shyly from behind the jagged outline of a ben.

"*Pâle étoile du soir* —" says Tony softly. "Do you know that thing, Hester?"

"Yes, and I love it. Why is it that one star is so much more beautiful than many?"

"One woman is much more beautiful than many," replies Tony. "And so is one flower."

This idea would not appeal to Mrs. Loudon, and I give Tony a description of my struggles with my hostess in the flower-room. It suddenly seems safer to keep the conversation in a humorous vein.

"I want to take you to Gart-na-Druim some day," says Tony suddenly (at least the name sounds like that). "Mrs. Loudon wouldn't mind, would she? It would take us all day. We could lunch there."

"What is there to see?" I ask him with interest.

"The Western Sea," Tony replies. "Small waves lapping softly on white beaches, and small rugged islands and mountains stretching their feet into the sea. It's like no other place in the world, and you really must have one peep at the Western Sea before you go. What about to-morrow —"

"I think I could. Mrs. Loudon wouldn't mind."

"There's a farm that we used to go to when we were children," Tony continues. "I would like you to see it. It's quite a tiny place on the hillside, but it was a sort of Paradise to us. We just ran wild with the farmer's children — spent long days fishing or trekking about the hills. I'd like you to meet Alec — he farms the place himself now that his father is dead."

"Is it a big farm?"

"Oh no — just a tiny croft and the soil is poor. He ekes out an existence with fishing. I never knew anybody so contented with his lot as Alec Macdonald — he's always happy. He was with me in the war. I managed to get him into my company and of course he was splendid — I knew he would be. Even in the tightest place — and we were in one or two pretty tight places together — Alec was perfectly calm and cheerful. I always go and see him when I am in this part of the world; he likes talking over old times."

The light in the garden is thinning now, the hedges and the trees are lost in gloom, the little white faces of the pansies shine like earthly stars. A moth flies past, and blunders against the lighted window with a dull thump.

"Poor creature," says Tony. "It wanted to get at the light."

"The glass saved its life," I reply.

"But it wanted to get to the light — don't you understand, Hester?"

"It would only have singed its wings."

"Why shouldn't it singe its wings if it wanted to?" asks Tony earnestly. "Don't you think *that one glorious moment* when it feels itself at the very heart of its desire is worth a pair of singed wings?"

Tony is really very puzzling; I never know whether his words have some deep meaning beyond my ken, or whether he is merely talking nonsense on purpose to bewilder me.

"I think it has had a lucky escape," I reply sternly, "and I hope it has learnt a lesson not to go chasing after lights in that idiotic way."

"I hope it hasn't," says Tony Morley softly.

There is a little silence. I can just see the gleam of his white shirt-front in the darkness and the fitful glow of his cigarette.

Suddenly Guthrie appears and says they have finished the rubber, and will Tony come and make up another four.

Tony replies that he is very comfortable where he is, and that he doesn't much care for bridge. "The only bridge worth playing is three-handed bridge," he adds didactically.

Guthrie, surprised and annoyed at this unusual preference, says that most people consider three-handed bridge too much of a gamble.

"That's what I like about it," says Tony, and I can tell he is smiling by the tone of his voice. "I like a gamble, and I like to gamble on my own. I like playing every hand myself. Partners are such a bore; they don't return your lead at the right moment, or they get fed up if you fail to bid in accordance with some twopenny-halfpenny convention."

"You must be very lucky if you are able to bid for dummy every time," Guthrie says, with cold fury.

Tony replies that he *is* lucky at cards, but not in love, and heaves a ridiculous sigh. "You should not grudge me that poor consolation, Loudon," he adds innocently.

Poor Guthrie turns on his heel, and disappears into the drawing-room without another word.

"Got him that time," says Tony with a short laugh.

"I don't know why you're such a beast to Guthrie," I tell him sternly.

"I don't know either," responds Tony thoughtfully, "except that the man has such rotten taste. He's going to have the devil of a life with that girl, and I'm sorry for him, and it annoys me frightfully to be sorry for people."

We return to the drawing-room and find the assembled company playing *vingt-et-un*, all except Mrs. Falconer, who says she is no good at arithmetic and never was. Room is made at the gambling table for Tony and me, and we make our stakes. Guthrie remarks that we shall now see whether Major Morley is lucky at cards, whereupon Tony produces an ace and a ten, and rakes in a pile of red counters with an amused smile.

The Bakers are the first to depart. Mr. Baker has been smothering huge yawns for some time, and casting anguished looks towards his daughter. I am thankful when at last she takes pity on him, for I feel that at any moment he may fall asleep in his chair, and have to be carried out to the car by Guthrie and Tony. They could accomplish this feat quite easily, of course, but Elsie would feel the indignity.

Mr. Baker pulls himself together at Elsie's signal, and thanks his hostess with suitable warmth for a delightful evening. "You must come and have dinner with Elsie and me at the Hotel," he says earnestly. "The food is first class — just tell the young people to fix a day."

Miss MacArbin says she thinks perhaps they should go home too.

"Well, if you really must —" says Mrs. Loudon. "Dobbie's ready when you are."

They all disappear, calling out that it has been a delightful evening and most enjoyable. Only Tony remains, and he and Guthrie repair to the dining-room for a last drink.

"It went off very well," says Mrs. Loudon as we turn out the lamps in the drawing-room and make our way upstairs. "Yon MacArbin girl is a pretty creature — I liked her. It's a lonely life for a young thing, keeping house for that brother — did you get any word with him, Hester? A dreigh sort of body, I thought."

"You seemed very much interested in his conversation at dinner," I point out.

"Anything to get away from that Baker man," she replies fervently. "The man scared me. Did you hear him havering on about his income as if it was settlements I was after? And, when I tried to shut him up about that, I declare to goodness he went on as if *I* was to marry *him* — told me I'd be driving him on a snaffle before long," adds Mrs. Loudon with a snort. "The cheek of the man, Hester! And yet it wasn't exactly cheek, either, for he was quite unconscious that he was saying anything wrong."

"Very difficult," I admit.

"Difficult!" she exclaims, as if I had insulted her by such under-estimation of her problem. "Difficult! I tell you, Hester, Torquemada's Crosswords are child's play compared to my situation with that man."

I feel too tired to discuss the party any further to-night, so I make my excuses to my hostess and retire to my room. I am just on the point of removing my earrings (Woolworth's Oriental Pearl) when I hear the sound of voices in the garden. Guthrie's voice, strangely harsh in tone, announces to some unseen companion:

"I know you think me a fool — I admit I'm no match for you, juggling with words — but I'm not a *cad*."

"What exactly do you mean by that, Loudon?" Tony's voice is smooth as silk.

(What a nuisance those two men are! I shall have to delay my undressing, in case it becomes necessary to go down and play the part of peacemaker. What do men *do* nowadays when they quarrel? I can't imagine them hitting each other, but perhaps this is only because I am entirely ignorant upon the subject. I think Tony would get the worst of it, if it came to blows — Guthrie's shoulders are so broad — yet I can't imagine a beaten and humiliated Tony. Somehow or other he would manage to come out on top.)

These thoughts fly through my head in a second. I blow out my candle, and lean out of the window. Evidently they are just below me, on the veranda, for the pungent scent of a cigar drifts up through the still air.

"Well, Loudon," says Tony's voice, after a short silence, "I am entitled to an explanation of your words."

There is a strangled curse from Guthrie. "You can always put me in the wrong if you like," he says furiously. "But I don't make love to other men's wives — I don't hang round like a damned lap-dog —"

(I realise at once that Guthrie must have discovered some episode of Tony's past — which is said in the Regiment to be of a lurid nature — or perhaps there is some "fairy" at the Hotel who has captured Tony's vagrant fancy. *I* have heard nothing about it, of course,

141

but the Bakers may have told Guthrie, or he may have found out in some other way. I have often noticed that men have a strange faculty for nosing out this sort of thing.)

To my surprise Tony does not seem very angry. He laughs, somewhat mirthlessly, and says:

"Oh, that's the trouble, is it? You need not worry; the lady is perfectly safe from me. She is hedged about with innocence."

"And if she were not?" Guthrie asks quickly.

"Oh, if she were not I would carry her off like old Hector MacQuill," is the calm reply.

They are now walking down the path towards the Bentley, and the scrunch of gravel drowns what Guthrie is saying, but Tony's answer comes quite clearly to my ears.

"That's my business," he says drily. "If I choose to singe my wings —"

I remember the moth blundering against the window, and the queer nonsense he talked about it — he was thinking of himself, I suppose, and his own affairs. What a strange, incomprehensible creature he is!

I realise that the crisis is past — for some reason they are not going to fight each other to-night. I heave a sigh of relief — for I am very tired — and crawl backwards out of my frock and hang it over a chair.

The Bentley departs, the angry voices have subsided, the night sinks into velvet peace. I kneel at my window and gaze up into the sky — a deep blue, glowing canopy above the dark, lacy branches of the firs. The stars glimmer like tiny yellow lamps. There is no sound save the silver tinkle of the burn, and, far off amongst the hills, a lamb bleats once and is quiet.

SATURDAY: 11TH JUNE

BETTY IS LOST — WE VISIT GART-NA-DRUIM

I jump out of bed and poke my head out of the window. There is a thick mist on the ground, and half-way up the hills, above the mist, floats the hill top, crested with trees, like a fairy island in a lake of fleecy wool.

This is the day of my expedition with Tony, he is to call for me at ten, and the problem which confronts me is this — what am I to wear? It all depends upon what sort of a day it is going to be. Will the mist clear off, or will it thicken and spread? Will it resolve into rain or lift into sunshine?

Guthrie is very cross at breakfast — there is no other word for it. He eats his kidneys with a glowering face, and nearly bites my head off when I enquire what kind of a day it is going to be. Meanwhile Mrs. Loudon smiles to herself as if she has some secret cause for amusement which nobody else may share.

Seeing that my companions are occupied with their own thoughts — pleasant or otherwise — I too relapse into silence, and commune with mine.

After some minutes the silence becomes leaden, like the stillness of a storm before it breaks, and, looking up, I see that Guthrie's mood has changed, his eyes are fixed upon me beseechingly — he is sorry.

I feel drawn to experiment with Guthrie — what will happen if I do not speak to this poor young man in a kind manner? Will he blow up and burst into a thousand pieces with the effort to contain his feelings, to keep all the things he wants to say locked up in his poor helpless body? Or will he merely finish his toast and marmalade and walk out of the room? What an alluring experiment it would be! But, alas, I cannot make it, for Mrs. Loudon is looking at me with pleading eyes. "Speak to him kindly," they seem to say. "Speak to him kindly for my sake. For if he should blow up into a thousand pieces, where should I find another son?"

I cannot resist such an appeal, so I lean forward and say very sweetly:

"Are you going to fish to-day, Guthrie?"

A sunbeam struggles through the clouds. "How can I without my ghillie?" he asks, half smiling, half sulky. "Don't go, Hester; we haven't got many days left. Why do you want to go dashing over the countryside, when we can spend a long day on the loch?"

"Don't be selfish, Guthrie," says Mrs. Loudon, and the wicked woman actually winks at me from behind her barrier of tea-cosies. "You can get Donald to row the boat if you want to fish — though you know perfectly well that you'll not catch anything with this mist all over everything. Of course Hester must go about, and see all she can of the country while she's here."

"She won't see much of it to-day — and *I* could have taken her if she had *said* she wanted to go. I haven't got a *Bentley*, of course," mutters Guthrie.

The owner of the Bentley now appears upon the scene and asks if I am ready. I reply cheekily that he is far too early, and that anybody who was not blind could see that I am still eating toast and marmalade and drinking coffee.

"Hurry up then, Mrs. Impudence," says Tony, with a smile.

Guthrie glowers.

"What kind of a day is it going to be?" asks Mrs. Loudon, looking up from her paper. "The weather news says — cloudy and unsettled, some mist locally, occasional sunshine."

"It seems a bit thundery to me," replies Tony, with a glance in Guthrie's direction.

At this moment the door opens, and discloses Annie — white-faced and breathless.

"Miss Betty's gone," she says.

"Gone!" cries Guthrie.

"I left her in the nursery while I took down the breakfast-tray, and when I got back she wasn't there —"

"She's hiding from you," Tony suggests anxiously.

"I thought she was at first," Annie admits, suddenly dissolving into tears. "But I've looked everywhere — and her coat and hat's gone too."

Something clutches at my heart, and the room swings round — Betty lost — Betty out alone in this horrible mist.

Tony's hand grips my shoulder. "Don't worry, Hester," he says quietly. "She won't have gone far — we'll soon find her —"

"Pull yourself together, Annie," says Mrs. Loudon in a firm, sensible voice. "It's not the slightest use weeping like that — try to think of something she said that might help us to find her — perhaps she has gone down to Donald's cottage to play with that boy of his."

"It was kelpies she was after," cries Annie, wringing her hands. "She's been talking about them ever since Mr. Guthrie told her that they lived in the streams — and this morning she said, 'Annie, it's just the sort of day to see a kelpie.'"

Guthrie's face is like a ghost. "My God!" he whispers. "What possessed me to tell her such a thing?"

"She'll have gone up the path by the burn side," Mrs. Loudon says.

"I know," he replies.

The two men rush out into the hall and seize their coats.

"Sit down, Hester," says Mrs. Loudon. "You'll only hinder them; they'll be far quicker themselves. Annie, pull yourself together for mercy's sake — tell Dobbie I want him, and send Jean down the garden for Donald and the garden boy —"

The house is full of bustle, and everyone seems to be doing something except me. I wander round the house and stare out of each window in turn. There is nothing to be seen but a thick white blanket of mist; a few branches of trees stick through it in a peculiar manner as if they had no trunks. The fence has disappeared.

147

Oh, Betty, where are you? What will Tim say when he hears I have lost Betty?

Mrs. Falconer comes down the stairs, and corners me in the hall before I have time to escape into the dining-room. By this time my nerves are frayed, and I am in no condition to cope with the woman. If she starts making fatuous remarks I shall scream; if she sympathises with me I shall weep. Fortunately for us both Mrs. Falconer does neither the one nor the other, and, for the second time in my acquaintance with her, I wonder whether she is really quite so foolish as she seems.

"Things always turn up," she says vaguely, more as if we were in the middle of a conversation about lost umbrellas than as if she were condoling with a bereft mother. "I'm always losing things myself, so I know. Why don't you look about yourself, my dear," she adds, peering shortsightedly beneath the hall-table, and motioning towards the umbrella stand. "Things never seem so lost when you're looking for them. I remember when I lost my gold locket which I always wear round my neck (it has some hair in it, you know, and I felt quite naked without it — although, of course, I had on all my clothes as usual). I had to keep on looking for it all the time, and I must have looked down the back of the drawing-room sofa at least nineteen times before Susan found it under the mat in the bath-room — but I just kept on looking for it, although I knew it wasn't there, because the moment I stopped looking for it I felt it was so much more lost."

"Yes," I reply, with a slight lightening of gloom.

"So just put on your hat and your mackintosh," continues the amazing woman. "You won't need an umbrella because the mist is really lifting a little (there was quite an orange patch in it where the sun is, when I looked out of my window just now), and take a turn round the garden. Poke amongst the rhododendrons with a stick or something — you'll feel *much* better if you just keep on looking —"

And the extraordinary thing is that she's right. I poke about the garden, and I feel better; the mist is white and thick, but it does not seem quite such a hopeless blanket as it did when viewed from the windows. So I poke amongst the rhododendrons, and peer over the gate into the woods and I wander blindly into the fruit garden, and shake the gooseberry bushes so that the mist, which has gathered on their leaves like diamonds, falls to the ground in showers.

Hours seem to pass, and then quite suddenly I notice that the mist is thinner — I feel a slight breath of air upon my cheek. Trees, that were invisible before, now loom up like shadows in my path, their dark, dripping foliage spreads above me like a drift of smoke. I grope my way back to the house, and Mrs. Loudon meets me at the door. She tries to smile at me, but her face is grey and drawn:

"There you are, Hester," she says, with a nervous laugh. "I was thinking we'd have to be sending out a search party for *you* next. It's certainly lifting," she adds.

149

The mist seems to be flowing now, eddying a little round the house; it moves slowly past like pieces of torn cotton wool.

"There," says Mrs. Loudon suddenly. "I thought I heard something — what's that?"

We stand very still, listening, and sure enough a faint shout comes to our ears. I cling to Mrs. Loudon's arm.

"It's all right, Hester," she says anxiously. "They wouldn't be shouting unless they had found the wee lamb — they wouldn't be coming back at all unless they had found her, if I know anything about either of them —"

It is true, of course, but I can't help trembling. She may easily have fallen over some rocks.

We stand there, peering out into the mist for what seems hours, and, at last, two dark figures loom up into sight.

"It's all right," cries Tony's voice. "We've got them; they're quite safe."

I see now that Guthrie and Tony are both carrying children.

"Goodness me, there's two of them!" murmurs Mrs. Loudon as they come up the path.

"It's Ian," says Tony. "They went together to find a kelpie — they're quite safe, only tired and cold —"

By this time Guthrie has bundled Betty into my arms, and I feel her cold, wet hands round my neck. We carry the wanderers into the morning-room, where there is a huge fire, and peel off their wet clothes. Everybody seems to be talking at once, but it is all hazy to me. I sit in front of the fire hugging Betty, and nothing matters at all except that she is safe. Mrs. Loudon bustles about getting hot soup and cherry brandy, and telling everybody to drink it up at once. "There's nothing better for keeping out the cold," she says. "But if anybody would rather have whisky, it's here."

"It was rather fun at first," Betty announces, sipping her hot soup, and stretching out a cold bare foot to the fire. "And then we got lost, and it was horrid, and then Guthrie came, and it was all right."

"It was frightfully naughty," I tell her in a shaking voice.

"But we wanted to see a kelpie — and Ian took his net to catch it — fancy if we had caught a darling little kelpie, Mummie."

"Someone had better let Ian's mother know that he's all right," suggests Tony. "I'll go, shall I?"

"You will not, then," replies Mrs. Loudon firmly. "I'll send Jean. Drink up your cherry brandy, Ian. Yes, I know it's hot; boys who go looking for kelpies in the mist deserve to get their insides burnt."

"They were up the burn, nearly as far as the Tarn," Tony is saying.

"Near that big heap of rocks," adds Guthrie.

"Loudon found them," says Tony, giving honour where honour is due.

"It was the Major's idea, though —" puts in Guthrie modestly. "Have some more brandy, sir."

"Thanks, I will," replies Tony, helping himself.

The atmosphere is positively genial, which is most unusual, and I only hope it will last. I hug Betty tightly

151

and rejoice silently in the feel of her soft body. She has been very naughty, of course, but I am so thankful to have her back, safe and sound, that I haven't the heart to scold her seriously.

"Major Morley, your feet are soaking," says Mrs. Loudon suddenly.

"I know," he replies. "It doesn't matter —"

"I'll find you some socks," Guthrie says. "My shoes will be too big, but still —"

Tony laughs, but allows himself to be persuaded into changing, and follows Guthrie upstairs.

"Those men!" says Mrs. Loudon, laughing. "They'll be at each other's throats again to-morrow, I suppose."

The excitement dies down in spite of Mrs. Falconer's efforts to fan the flame. By lunch-time everything seems normal, and I can hardly believe that anything has happened. The mist has vanished, and the sun blazes down on to a green and golden world. Betty is none the worse for her adventure, and eats largely of mince collops, a Scottish dish in which she delights.

"I wish we had seen a kelpie," says Betty, with a sigh, as she hands in her plate for a second helping.

Guthrie looks across the table at her with a grave face. "There aren't any to see. There are no such things as kelpies, Betty, so don't you go looking for them any more."

"But you told me —" says Betty.

"I know — but it was all nonsense," Guthrie replies. "I shouldn't have told you — it was just made up."

"No kelpies!" says Betty, her lip quivering.

"No kelpies!" replies Guthrie firmly.

"But we can have stories about kelpies, can't we?"

"Och, let the child be!" whispers Mrs. Loudon.

"No," says Guthrie firmly. "I made up my mind that if we found her safely — I mean I made up my mind out there on the moor that I wouldn't tell Betty anything that wasn't true — never again — and I mean to stick to it. If Betty wants stories we can have stories about dogs, or — or elephants, or something —"

Betty looks at him, and he looks at Betty, gravely, seriously; and it seems to me that in spite of Betty's youth she understands a little of what Guthrie has gone through. Something precious has come into being between those two, something deeper and far more lasting than their former irresponsible friendship.

"I think," says Mrs. Loudon suddenly. "I think it would be a good plan if we all went over to Inverquill this afternoon, to the pictures; it would take our minds off —"

"What about our expedition?" says Tony, looking at me persuasively.

"Goodness me, I'd forgotten all about it!" exclaims Mrs. Loudon. "It's not too late for you to start now. Away with you before the day's any older."

I feel that I would really rather stay with Betty, but can think of no excuse that does not sound foolish. Betty will be perfectly safe and happy to go to the Picture House at Inverquill with the others. While I am still wondering what to say, the whole thing is settled — Mrs. Loudon is an adept at arranging other people's affairs, and has a strange compelling force. I can't

153

explain it except by saying that you find yourself carrying out her behests without intending to do so.

Tony and I are hustled off without more ado, and are soon tucked up in the Bentley and flying along the moorland roads like the wind. The day is all golden now, bright golden sunshine pours down from a sky dappled with soft clouds.

"You don't mind going fast?" Tony says suddenly. "We haven't much time, and it would be rather nice to bathe, wouldn't it?"

I agree that it would be lovely. I don't mind going fast with Tony; he is one of those born drivers who give you a feeling of complete safety however fast they go.

He says no more, but fixes his attention on the road. His profile, only, is visible to me as I turn my head in his direction. There is something stern and sad about this view of his face — the straight nose, and the straight lips, compressed into a thin line with the concentration of his thoughts. I realise how little I know about Tony. I know him so well in some ways, but the inward Tony is a mysterious creature; kind and impish, sorrowful and gay by turns, and the mainspring of these changing moods is hidden deep.

The car flies on, over moors, through forests, past lochs which sleep peacefully in the sun; now it lifts over the shoulder of a hill, now it winds along by the side of a river. We seem to have been travelling for hours.

We climb a long, steep hill, and stop for a moment at the top. Far below us lies the sea, shimmering in the sunlit mist. It holds my eyes to the exclusion of all else as the sea always must. The sun is piercing the mist with golden beams, making it opalescent as a rainbow. These shafts of sunlight make pools of light upon the gently heaving bosom of the sea.

Now we are running slowly down the hill to the sea's edge: to our left is a pile of rocks, capped by green turf and a cluster of fir trees; it thrusts its feet out into the sea, sheltering a little bay where the sand is silvery white. Turf of emerald brightness, starred with tiny flowers, edges the bay, and stretches back to the hills, where the young larches stand in patterns of pale green flame against the smoky shadows of the pines. The sea is trembling as the mist lifts and eddies, the gleaming patches of sunlight spread and merge, and their surface is ruffled by a faint breeze from the west. Far off, and blue in the haze, float the tall forms of islands, some rugged and sterile, others crowded with trees to the water's edge. Just at our feet a spit of silvery sand runs out into the shimmering water. It is crowned with reeds which rustle gently in the faintly stirring air. The whole scene is fairy-like in quality, there is something unearthly in its soft beauty, in its stillness, and the delicacy of its colouring; every shade of colour, from the silvery whiteness of the sand to the darkest shadows of the pines is caught and blended into a perfect whole.

"This is my favourite bay," says Tony softly. "Shall we bathe here?"

"I can't believe the sea is real enough to bathe in."

"Oh, it's quite wet, I assure you. There's rather a nice little sandy cave amongst the rocks where you can undress."

155

He takes our two bundles out of the car and leads the way. I follow in a kind of dream — it is too beautiful to be real.

The sandy cave is a delightful place; it has little pink flowers in its crevices, and tall pine trees leaning over the top. I undress in comfort, and don my bathing-suit with the scent of the pines in my nostrils and the murmur of their foliage in my ears.

Tony is waiting for me on the rocks. He has been in already, and his fair hair is streaked with wetness, and shining with little drops of water.

"Come on," he says, smiling happily. "It's cold at first, but glorious —"

The water is almost still. It is very green, and so clear that the sand at the bottom is clearly visible, and a shoal of tiny fish, some silver and some red, dart in and out of the gently moving seaweed. We plunge in off the rocks. I let myself sink down to the bottom, and then spring up to the surface for a breath of air.

The sun is quite warm now. We sit dripping on the shore, and watch the seagulls diving for fish far out amongst the fairy islands.

"Do you like it, Hester?" Tony asks.

"I like it so much I can't talk about it. It's perfect. I should like to live here always, and sleep in the little cave, and watch the dawn break over the hills, and the sun set in the sea behind the islands."

We slip back once more into the clear water, and become part of its radiant life. It is so easy to float on its cool surface, to turn over like a lazy porpoise, and feel the salty buoyancy of its embrace. The waves are small and timid; they creep along the base of the rocks and fall with tiny splashes upon the white sand of the bay.

I dress in a leisurely manner, and feel the glorious heat rushing through my body and tingling in every nerve.

"Hurry up, Hester," shouts Tony. "Are you dressing for a Drawing-room at Buckingham Palace, or have you lost the feminine equivalent of a collar-stud in the sand?"

"I've lost nothing — except about ten years," I reply, emerging from my lair, and wringing out my bathing-dress.

"So you have," agrees Tony, looking at me in what I feel to be a peculiar manner. "You aren't a day older than Betty. I've always thought seven was the most attractive age."

I beseech him not to be foolish, and he replies that he will give the matter his attention. By this time we have stowed the wet bathing-dresses and the sandy towels in the car, and are walking up the hill to visit the farm. I find it impossible to talk. There is too much to see, and I want to remember it all — every smallest detail — so that I may store it forever in "that inward eye which is the bliss of solitude." Look where you will, a different kind of country opens up before you. Here, in the space of half a mile, you have the sea with its rocks and sands, and innocent shimmer of scarcely moving water; the pinewoods, close and tightly packed together, their foliage like drifts of green smoke above their straight boles; the delicate green of birch and larch; the meadow land, all starred with tiny flowers; and the patchwork quilt of fields spread upon the sloping hills. From the bosom of a meadowy hill, a strong young burn leaps out and rushes seaward; a little wooden bridge carries the path across the water and sets it on its way. There is a wooden rail — grey with age, and yellow with lichen — which we lean upon, watching the silver wave of water as it meets the rocks in its bed, and parts to squeeze between them, or spreads over their rounded surfaces like a fan of clear brown wine.

The little white croft upon the hill is sheltered from the north by a grove of trees. In front is a cobbled yard, and a large green tub of rain-water stands by the door. A faint reek of peat-smoke rises from the chimney and fills the air with its attractive smell.

"Hullo, hullo! Are you there, Alec?" shouts Tony as we approach.

The door flies open, and a man appears, a tall, broad-shouldered man. He has the brown weather-beaten face and far-sighted eyes of one who spends his time upon the sea, and the earth-engrained hands of a farmer — for Alec is both.

"Och, Major!" he cries. "Is it yourself? It's welcome you are."

They shake hands firmly. "Och, well now!" he says, beaming with happiness. "This is a fery good day."

Tony now introduces me, and I am included in the welcome. "Och, indeed now I would be remembering the captain (or will he be major now?), and it's a proud day for me to be welcoming his lady to my home."

"Oh, of course," Tony says. "I'd forgotten you had met Tim Christie."

"But *I* had not forgotten," Alec replies, with a smile. "It would be a strange thing if I would not be remembering *him*, for we were all together in the worst place I ever was in."

"That farm near Festubert," puts in Tony. "Yes, it was a tight place. Tim Christie was there, was he?"

"He was indeed," nods Alec. "I could be telling you at this moment all the people that were there. Perhaps I have more time for remembering than other people, for when I am out at night in my boat at the fishing I will be thinking again about all the things we would be doing at that time, and all the good times we would be having — for there were good times as well as bad."

"We didn't have much of a time at that farm," says Tony grimly.

"Och well, and I don't know, Major. I wouldn't have missed it now; for it's a grand thing to be thinking about it all, and you safe in your bed, or sitting by the fire, and the wind roaring round. There's times I feel sorry for the young men who are knowing nothing of it all, for it's half alive they are, and not knowing their luck to be that."

"That's one way of looking at the war!"

"Och well, it's my way," he says. "I would often be thinking of the adventure of it all, and the foreign lands, and the strange things that I would be seeing those times —"

"That German soldier you met in the communication trench, for instance," suggests Tony smiling.

"That one," says Alec with an answering grin. "It was a funny thing that. We were both of us frightened of the other one, not expecting to meet each other in that place. A young man he was, with a pleasant face — och, I'd like fine to be meeting him now, that one, and standing him a drink and laughing over the pair of us crawling along that place and bumping into each other — and we scared to death! But what am I doing to be keeping you standing out here? If you would be coming into my house —"

We follow him into the tiny living-room, which is spotlessly clean and shining. The walls are white-washed, and a kettle is singing on the open fire. A small child of about four years old is playing on the hearth-rug with a battered wooden train; he gives one loud shriek when he sees us and flies for his life.

"Mrs. Christie must forgive him," Alec says, setting chairs for us. "He sees nobody here, and he is shy. It is a lonely place, and —"

"I suppose you will want another war for him in twenty years or so," suggests Tony.

"The Major would be laughing at me," replies Alec smiling. "But no, I would be wanting no war for him. It is only that I am glad now there was one for me. I was not glad at the time, no, not altogether glad. Wars are bad things, and we want no more of them — but there is good in them for the lucky ones."

"I believe you are right," says Tony gravely.

Mrs. Macdonald now appears, and greets us shyly. She is a pretty young woman with dark hair and quiet eyes. Alec enquires after his son, somewhat anxiously.

"He will have gone to speak to the pig," replies his mother lightly. "There is no need whatever to be troubling ourselves about that one."

So we cease to trouble ourselves about young Macdonald, who has bad taste to prefer the pig's conversation to ours, and settle down to a comfortable chat. I am amazed to find my host so well-informed as to affairs. These people are far from civilisation, and cut off from the outer world, yet, in spite of this, Alec can hold his own with Tony, and gives his opinion on current topics — holding to his opinion with respectful firmness when Tony differs from him. They discuss the effect of tariffs, unemployment, and disarmament, while Mrs. Macdonald makes tea, and sets out large plates of scones and crisp home-made oatcakes on a snowy cloth. When all is ready the younger Alec is retrieved from the pigsty, and placed upon a high wooden chair to have his tea. But the tears roll down his cheeks whenever he looks at us, and at last I can bear it no longer and beseech his parents to take pity on him. "Couldn't he have his tea somewhere else?" I suggest.

"Och, he is a foolish boy!" says his mother. "He does not know when he is well off."

"He is not used to taking his tea with company present," adds his father.

"It's proud and happy he should be to be taking tea with a grand lady and gentleman," says his mother. But the younger Alec is so obviously neither proud nor happy that, at last, he is permitted to retire under the table to finish his meal. Alec is full of excuses for his

161

offspring, but Mrs. Macdonald is quite unperturbed, and, having given him his mug of milk — warm from the cow — and provided him with a large, jammy scone, she forgets all about him.

We leave the menfolk to their barren discussion anent disarmament, and discourse together about the more important matters of every day. I am interested to hear about Mrs. Macdonald's life, and she is interested in telling me. Gart-na-Druim is ten miles from the nearest village (or clachan) and the butcher only calls twice a week. Fortunately the farm is practically self-supporting; they have their own butter and eggs, of course, and plenty of fish when Alec can get time to catch them. Yes, it's lonely in the long dark winters — she comes from Oban way, and found it very quiet at first — sometimes the farm is cut off from the outer world for weeks at a time. There was a big snow three years ago, and they ran out of oil and candles. That wasn't very nice, Mrs. Macdonald says, because it was dark at four o'clock, and they just had to go to bed. Wee Alec was a baby then, and everything was very difficult. "But there was fun in it too," she adds, with a twinkle in her eye. "Alec took a bite of soap in the dark, he was thinking it was cheese — och, I'll not forget that in a hundred years! I could not be seeing his face, but I could be hearing what he was saying well enough. Well, after that, I am laying in a store of candles every winter."

"It must be lonely, when Alec is out all day," I suggest.

"Well, it is, then," she agrees. "It is lonely in the winter, but the summer is very nice. Alec's sisters come for their holidays — Alec's sisters are in good positions in Glasgow, they are very nice — and it is a wonder how the time will be flying past with all there is to do. It is just one thing and then another all day long. And wee Alec is a very nice companion now — it is not often he is foolish like to-day."

The men are still deep in talk, so Mrs. Macdonald offers to show me round the farm.

"Don't be long, Hester," says Tony, as he sees us depart. "We must start back in half an hour or Mrs. Loudon will be sending out a search-party."

I follow my hostess out of the door, and she shows me round with an air, half deprecating and half proud, which I find very attractive. She is indeed an attractive creature, with her dark hair and milky complexion. Her voice is low and soft, and she knows when to speak and when to be silent.

I feel that she is a little shy (from being so isolated from her kind) but there is no awkwardness in her manner. She is both simple and dignified, with the reserve of a great lady and the friendliness of a child.

"This a great day for Alec," she says, as we inspect the dairy, a small but spotlessly clean shed in the shadow of an overhanging rock. "I'll not be hearing the end of this day for long."

Small Alec follows us timidly; he is a beautiful child, and I am able to praise his looks to his mother with an easy conscience.

"Och, he's well enough," she replies, looking down at her son with adoring pride. "He's well enough if his father would not be wasting him the livelong day. His father is thinking there's no child in the world but him, and it's trouble enough I have with the two of them, so it is."

My efforts to speak to Alec, the younger, meet with blank looks, and I conclude that he is still too frightened of me to reply to my blandishments.

"Do not be troubling about him, Mrs. Christie," says his mother. "He is not very good at the English yet; it is the Gaelic we do be speaking to him."

I try him with a bar of chocolate, which I discover in the pocket of my coat, and find, to my delight, that he seems to understand this quite easily and to know exactly what to do with it.

The cows are grazing on a steep piece of pasture land upon the hill, but we inspect their byre. We then move on to another shed, from whence issues a strange smell of burning and clouds of smoke. Mrs. Macdonald opens the door, and reveals rows of fish hanging on lines across a smouldering fire — it is here that she cures the fish ready for the market in the city. I have often eaten kippers and smoked fish, of course, but I never realised that this was the way they were prepared — I never even wondered how they became kippers and smoked fish, though I suppose I must have known, if I had thought about the matter seriously, that they could not have come out of the sea in that condition.

The pigsty is our next stop. There is something about the pink nakedness of a pig that revolts me. I could never extend my friendship to a pig, however sweet its disposition might be. But little Alec is of a different mind. He speaks to it in fond accents quite unintelligible to me, and the pig (obviously a Celtic pig) lifts its ugly snout and grunts back at him.

"Indeed she is all but human," says Mrs. Macdonald indulgently, and I realise, quite suddenly, that this is one of the reasons I don't like her.

It is now my turn to be informative, so we sit down on a log of wood in the warm sunshine, and I try to answer Mrs. Macdonald's questions about life in the Army. I tell her about the married families and their communal existence, and how they move from place to place as they follow the drum. I tell her about India — the heat, and the hordes of native servants and the great troopships packed with women and children. She listens with wide eyes, and sometimes she says: "That would be very nice, so it would," and sometimes she says, with a little cry of horror, "Och, that would not be nice at all!" So the time passes very pleasantly, and wee Alec plays round the yard, and falls down and hurts himself and is comforted with strange soft words, and runs off to play again.

Tony and Alec are now seen approaching, and I realise that it is getting late. With great difficulty we refuse more tea — this time with kippers — Mrs. Macdonald declares that she could have it ready in a moment. Fortunately, Tony is clever enough to refuse it without hurting our hostess's feelings, and I feel — not for the first time — that Tony should have been an

165

ambassador; his diplomacy has been wasted as a mere major in His Majesty's Army.

We tear ourselves away, and big Alec walks down the hill with us to see us start. He is going out fishing to-night, for the gulls diving in the bay are indicative of a shoal of fish; he points out his boat, which is rocking lazily in a small cove at the mouth of the burn.

"A good night for it," Tony says. "I wish I could come out with you, Alec."

"I wish you could then, Major," replies Alec fervently.

Once more the sea has changed, and long rollers are coming in from the west, long lazy rollers, with the sun glinting on their glassy slopes. The sky is blue, tinged with palest mauve, and far away behind the islands there is a bank of purple cloud.

"It's blowing up," Tony says.

"It is, then," agrees Alec. "I will be trying for them off the Black Rock to-night — you will be remembering the Black Rock, Major?"

"We always got a basket there."

"Och, those were days! I would like wee Alec to have days like those —"

Tony says: "Well, good luck to the fishing, Alec."

There is a deep undercurrent of feeling beneath the bald simplicity of their words. They understand each other — these two — as only those who have shared pleasures and hardships can understand each other. Memories, grave and gay, bind them together in a comradeship which needs no words, no outward expression; a comradeship more faithful than love, more lasting than life.

Soon we are breasting the steep hill, leaving behind us the sea, the white sands, and the cluster of dark pines. I look back and wave to Alec — a dwindling figure on the white road with the sun shining on his bared head — then we pass over the crest of the hill, and the valley disappears.

To-day has revealed still another Tony — the Tony that Alec knows and worships — perhaps this is the real Tony at last.

167

SUNDAY: 12TH JUNE

GUTHRIE READS THE PAPERS — MRS. MACTURK CALLS AND IS DISCOMFITED BY MRS. FALCONER

It is a hot, stuffy, thundery sort of afternoon — too hot to do anything except lie in a deck-chair. The ladies have retired to their rooms saying they had letters to write, but I feel convinced they are both dreaming peacefully upon their beds. Only Betty seems to have any energy. She declares her intention of bathing in the loch, and hops off, followed by the faithful Annie bearing bath-towels.

Guthrie is reading the Sunday paper, which has just arrived — I look at him, and marvel that anyone can find the affairs of the world so important on a hot Sunday afternoon. Papers are tiring things to read at the best of times, they make your arms ache, and you can usually pick up the most interesting pieces of news from the general conversation.

"'Organdie has come into its own,'" reads Guthrie solemnly. "How interesting that is! Who or what is organdie, Hester? 'Lady Furbelow wore a charming frock of Old Tile, with a partridge cowl (good heavens, is it a woman or a bungalow they're describing?). The

168

Honourable Mrs. Killjoy had chosen ginger *lainage* with chestnut trimmings for her *ensemble* (makes me think of Christmas). The Countess of Nockhem was gowned in foam (how cold she must have been!). She carried an afternoon pochette in Nile rayon. Her daughter was charming in Mallard crêpe with a Sahara cape and gauntlets. (In other words she was a duck in the desert.) Mrs. Deff Mewte chose sage (but not onions) — how lucky she is to be a *true* platinum blonde!"

I can't help laughing feebly at his disgusted expression.

"But really, Hester," he says seriously. "Who on earth writes tripe like that? They ought to be drowned. It's simply *awful*, and on the next page you read 'Young Girl Murdered on a Yorkshire Moor, Doctor's Examination Reveals — ' Ah, hum, yes — very sad —"

I make horrified noises; it is really much too hot to argue with Guthrie. The sun blazes down. Silence falls. Presently the paper, with its curious items of news, slips on to the ground with a soft rustle — Guthrie is asleep and I am not far off it.

Suddenly I open my eyes and see Jean coming towards us across the lawn, followed by a large bulgy figure in white lace — for a moment I think that I am dreaming, but only for a moment. Mrs. MacTurk is too substantial to be the figment of a dream. I have only time to kick Guthrie on the shin — perhaps rather harder than I intend — before composing my face into a false smile and going forward to greet her.

169

Guthrie leaps to his feet with a muffled curse — it is extraordinary how quickly he wakes — and gazes about him in bewilderment.

"Naughty, naughty," says Mrs. MacTurk, wagging her finger at me in a skittish manner as she totters up to me on her spike-like heels. "You've been here ten days and never come over to see us. Mr. MacTurk is quite hurt."

Guthrie is still in a dazed condition, and evidently imagines that this is one of my bosom friends. "I'm sure if Mother had known —" he says, offering her his chair. "I'm afraid we've been very selfish with Hester — fishing and all that — we've kept her all to ourselves. But you must stay to tea. Mother will be down quite soon, and she will be delighted to see you. We must arrange something — fishing or — or something."

Mrs. MacTurk beams at him. "And you must *all* come to dinner at the Hotel with Mr. MacTurk and I," she says hospitably. "Mr. MacTurk will order a special dinner for you — it doesn't matter to us how many of you there are."

This wholesale invitation takes Guthrie slightly aback. He looks at me for guidance, whereupon I immediately signal "wash-out," still smiling brightly at our unexpected visitor. This signal has proved most valuable to Tim and myself on similar occasions, and I can only hope that the same code of signals obtains in the Senior Service.

"That's very kind," Guthrie says. "*Very* kind indeed, only Mother scarcely ever goes out to dinner nowadays — and we have an old cousin staying with us just now," he drops his voice confidentially, "a *widow*, you know — so *sad* —"

"But *you* will come — er — *Captain* Loudon," says Mrs. MacTurk persuasively. "You and Mrs. Christie, and any other young people that you like. Mr. MacTurk will send the Rolls for you any evening. We've got to know some cheery people at the Hotel, and it really would be a cheery evening. Mr. Stuart Thompson is a real comic — you should see him take off the head waiter, and we can have Miss Baker too — I know *she's* a friend of yours."

It is at this moment, when Guthrie and I are at our wits' end for some plausible excuse, that Mrs. Falconer appears upon the horizon. She looks fresh and bright, and has, quite obviously, had a refreshing snooze. We signal to her like shipwrecked mariners, and she comes towards us, tripping lightly over the grass.

"Oh!" she exclaims. "How very interesting to meet you, Mrs. MacTaggart! I wonder if you are related to some perfectly delightful people — great friends of my parents — who used to live at Brighton. They had a large estate in Scotland, of course, but *he* was rather a delicate man and the doctors advised Brighton. We used to call upon them whenever we went there — which was pretty frequently because Mama found the air so beneficial to her asthma. Mama was not very strong, and was quite unable to chaperon us girls to the balls, so we used to go with Mrs. MacTaggart and her daughters. We were all so amused on one occasion when a gentleman came up to her and asked if we were

171

all her daughters. 'There is a great family resemblance, Madame,' he said. *How* we laughed! For of course *we* were not related to her at all. It is so strange that nowadays girls do not require chaperons. I often wonder how they have the courage to walk into the ball-room by themselves. I heard a very ridiculous story the other day about a chaperon and a curate. I can't remember what it was *she* said to *him*, but he replied something about a dodo — comparing her to a dodo. Probably her appearance reminded him of the picture of the dodo in *Alice in Wonderland*. It was an excellent story, we all laughed heartily, I remember. Papa always used to say 'laugh and grow fat' — I dare say *you* are fond of a good laugh, Mrs. MacTaggart," says Mrs. Falconer, with an eye on our guest's ample proportions.

Mrs. MacTurk, slightly bewildered by Mrs. Falconer's sudden question, hesitates whether to disown her *embonpoint*, or stand for a sense of humour at all costs. She loses her opportunity of getting a word in edgeways.

"My brother, Edward, once had a fat white bull-terrier," says Mrs. Falconer reminiscently, and it is only too obvious what has given rise to this new train of thought. Guthrie dives to collect the scattered newspapers with a strange choking cough.

"It was a most intelligent animal," Mrs. Falconer continues. "Guthrie dear, have you swallowed a fly or something?"

"No, yes," says Guthrie. "At least, I think it was a bull-terrier."

"A bull-terrier! My dear boy, how could you possibly have swallowed a bull-terrier? It must have been a gnat."

I have been watching our guest with great interest; her reactions to Mrs. Falconer's conversation are worthy of note. She was first annoyed, then incredulous, and then utterly bewildered. I can now see her staggering like a torpedoed ship.

Tea appears, and with it our hostess, clad as usual in her shabby garments and queenly manner. Her manner becomes even more queenly when she perceives Mrs. MacTurk, whom she abhors.

"How do you do?" she enquires stiffly, and is compelled by her old-fashioned notion of hospitality to shake the woman's hand.

Mrs. MacTurk, already sinking under the waves of Mrs. Falconer's talk, is in no condition to do herself justice. She replies feebly that she is well, and relapses into silence.

The fortunes and misfortunes of the bull-terrier — which rejoiced in the name of Hannibal — are now related to us by Mrs. Falconer with a wealth of detail rarely equalled and never surpassed. We pull it through distemper in 1898, follow it to the seaside with the family in 1899, and finally attend its tragic demise — through eating rat poison — in 1902. Hannibal is buried in the garden with Christian honours beneath the shade of an elm, and his virtues are commemorated by a stone for which the whole family subscribe their monthly pence. From this sad scene we proceed by an agile bound to Mrs. Falconer's recollections of a visit to

Madame Tussaud's. Here Mama accosts the wax policeman, and asks him the way to the Chamber of Horrors, while Papa, as usual, improves the occasion with well-chosen aphorisms.

Tea is now over, and we move slowly round the garden to the front drive, where the Rolls is waiting with its mulberry-coloured chauffeur in attendance. Mrs. MacTurk suddenly realises that this is her last chance, and makes a wild effort to gain her hostess's ear.

"Mr. MacTurk and I are staying at the Hotel," she says breathlessly, and I can see the invitation to dinner is trembling upon her lips, but Mrs. Falconer pounces on the last word like a tiger.

"At the *Hotel!*" she exclaims. "I wonder if you have met a friend of Guthrie's who is staying there just now — Major Morley his name is. He is really a very nice man, though a trifle too scurrilous for my liking."

"Scurrilous!" gasps Mrs. MacTurk.

"It just means very talkative," explains Mrs. Falconer kindly. "Dear Papa used such *long* words, and us girls got into the habit of saying them, just from hearing *him* — much to Mama's horror. Poor Mama was always telling us we would never get husbands if we used such long words. It was not fashionable to be clever in my young days. Poor dear Mama was always telling us about it. 'Let your conversation be yea yea and nay nay' she used to say. That's out of the Bible, of course, so I've no doubt it is very good advice, but if we all did that, and went about saying 'yea yea and nay nay' we should look rather silly, and there would not be any conversation at all. Papa's views upon the subject were not quite so extreme; he used to say that conversation should never be one-sided. There should be give and take about it, and I think that is so *true*. And that is why I really do not care very much for Major Morley," adds Mrs. Falconer triumphantly.

By this time Mrs. MacTurk's eyes are quite glassy, and, when the mulberry chauffeur opens the door of the car, she gets in like a woman walking in her sleep, and is whirled off down the drive without saying another word.

"How very strange not to say 'Good-bye,'" says Mrs. Falconer, peering down the drive after the disappearing Rolls with her shortsighted eyes. "Did you notice that, Elspeth? Guthrie, did *you* notice? People *are* extraordinary nowadays. Papa always said —"

But Mrs. Loudon does not remain to hear Papa's ideas upon the subject — she is already hastening into the house; and Guthrie is making for the woods as if he were fleeing from the wrath to come. I murmur that I *must* write some letters at once, and follow my hostess with all speed. Mrs. Falconer is left standing on the drive, the unconscious victor of the day, in undisputed possession of all she surveys.

I find Mrs. Loudon in the drawing-room, sitting on the sofa and giggling feebly.

"Gracious me!" she gasps. "Did you see the poor body's face? I declare to goodness I was sorry for the woman — though I can't thole her! She'll be away back to the Hotel with the story that I've a tame lunatic in the house."

We discuss the afternoon's entertainment at length, dwelling on the parts which appealed particularly to our sense of humour.

"'Yea yea and nay nay!'" exclaims Mrs. Loudon, with a gust of laughter. "Poor Millie, it's a crime to laugh at her, but the thing's beyond me this time."

"How could she help being peculiar with parents like that?" I reply. "Poor Mama was a harmless idiot, of course, but I feel sure I would have hated dear Papa."

"You would not, then," says Mrs. Loudon promptly. "Uncle Edward was a nice, kind, wise-like creature. That's just the odd bit. Millie doesn't exactly tell lies, but she makes everything sound different from what it was. Yon tale about the dog, for instance — I was staying with them when the beast died, and it all happened exactly as she said — and yet it was not like that at all."

"You should have been there when she began the story," I gasp, wiping my flowing tears. "She took one long look at Mrs. MacTurk, and away she went — I thought Guthrie would have burst."

"I'm thankful I missed that. It would have destroyed me," rejoins my hostess feebly. "The woman really is exactly like yon bulldog — even to her small beady eyes. I don't admire your taste in friends, Hester."

"I know you don't," I reply with sorrowful emphasis.

"Well, well!" says Mrs. Loudon, rising and blowing her nose with a trumpeting sound. "Well, well, it's been a mad sort of tea-party, and I dare say it's very good for us to have a good laugh, but I'll not get any letters written sitting here giggling with you —"

176

"I thought you were writing letters all the afternoon."

"It was too hot," she replies. "I just sat down by the window with a book, and the next thing I knew it was tea-time. And if an old done woman can't take a nap on a Sunday afternoon without people grinning at her like a Cheshire cat I don't know what the world's coming to. Away with you, I *must* write Elinor before dinner. Did you know Elinor Bradshaw, by any chance, when you were at Hythe?" she continues, rummaging fiercely in her desk. "Elinor's perhaps coming up for a few days towards the end of the month."

"Good heavens, are they still there?" I exclaim, pausing on my way to the door.

Mrs. Loudon laughs. "There speaks the wanderer. And why shouldn't they still be there in their own comfortable house? It's not everyone goes trailing over the face of the world like you soldiers' wives. Elinor's still there in the same place, and there's no reason to suppose she will leave it till she's carried out feet first. I don't know why I asked if you knew them, except that they always seem to have a stream of Army friends coming and going about the house. Elinor is forever in despair about some bosom friend or other going off to India or Aldershot or some such outlandish spot — and then another woman appears on the scene, and the first one's forgotten in a week."

As usual, Mrs. Loudon has hit off her subject to the life — I can't help laughing at the portrait. How incredible it seems that Elinor has been living there all this time, and I have never thought of her from one year's end to another! I have moved from place to place, borne children, ordered dinners, been happy or intensely miserable, and Elinor has lived on at Hythe keeping house for her brother, with no changes in her life, save the one sad change of growing older. How incredible it seems that the house, with its sunny aspect, and parquet floors, and the garden with its gorgeous roses and queer old sun-dial, are still the same! Although I have not thought of them for years they have been there all the time —

"But don't you think," says Mrs. Loudon, with a twinkle in her eye. "Don't you think you are a wee thing egotistical, Hester, to be surprised that the poor creatures can go on living unless you think of them occasionally?"

"You're a witch," I tell her, "and a black witch at that." And, with this parting shot, I leave her to write to Elinor, and fly upstairs to write to Tim.

MONDAY: 13TH JUNE

BETTY AND I VISIT THE SHOP AND WALK HOME WITH ELSIE BAKER

Betty and I decide to walk to the village. She wishes to spend a sixpence which she won from Guthrie, who bet her that she could not sit still for two minutes. We set off together very happily across the moor.

"I only did it by wriggling my toes," Betty informs me. "Two minutes is a terrible long time — I suppose it was quite *fair* to wriggle my toes?" she enquires anxiously.

The hill wind is cold, and whips our hair across our faces. The larch trees quiver, and bend their proud heads and shake their glittering leaves. The wind rustles through the pale green bracken, and flows over the moor like a crystal stream. The clouds are racing over the hills, there is movement everywhere to-day.

Betty finds a glossy-leaved plant with a golden flower — I don't know its name? Never mind, probably it has some long, clumsy, Latin name which does not suit it at all. Flowers should be born with names fitting to their beauty, not labelled by spectacled scientists with collecting tins and dissecting scissors; and those flocks of cloud, like teeming ewes rushing over the hills, they too have long names, according to their shape and density, but, to me, they are a flock of ewes, driven by the summer wind.

Betty runs, and jumps, and springs into the air like a young goat.

"The hills make me full of springiness," she says. "D'you think I shall find something nice to buy at the shop, Mummie? Guthrie says they have everything except what you want, but I don't know what I want so perhaps they'll have it. What do you think, Mummie?"

The problem is beyond me, and I say so with suitable humility.

"I like Guthrie — don't you?" she continues, hopping along on one leg. "But I like Major Morley much better. He's the cleverest, isn't he? Guthrie's rather stupid sometimes. And I like Mrs. Loudon, and I like Mrs. Falconer — *she* said I was to call her Aunt Millie, but I always forget. Why does she want me to call her Aunt Millie, Mummie? And I like Mary, and I like Kitty, but I don't like Jean. Don't you think Jean's got a cross face, Mummie? And Annie doesn't like Jean either. Annie says she gets the sulks."

We reach the village shop without adventure, and Betty turns her attention to the business in hand, while I invest in stamps and darning-wool.

"I think I'll buy a post-card for Daddy," she says. "And something for Annie — some chocolate perhaps. Oh, what a darling little pail! That red one — how much is it? Oh, dear, I've only got sixpence! Well, how much is that fishing-rod? — Oh, dear, haven't you got anything only sixpence? No, I don't want a ball —"

180

I have completed my modest purchases by this time, and am forced to go to Betty's aid. The shop is ransacked by a patient girl to find something that will appeal to my daughter, and yet be within her means. She seems to have forgotten her altruistic intentions towards Daddy and Annie. Boats, dolls, painting-books are all turned down; they do not attract her at all. I can't help wishing that it were not against my principles to buy her a fishing-rod — price half a crown — as it would solve all our difficulties in a trice; but I feel that this would be bad training for her character.

At last a wooden hoop is brought to light; Betty greets its appearance with rapture, and demands its price with bated breath. The patient girl replies glibly that it is "chust sixpence with the stick" and all is well.

Coming out of the shop we meet Elsie Baker, attired in the height of fashion, with a red cap on the very back of her head. She says she has been wanting to see me, and can she walk back a bit of the way with me? I reply that she can, and we set off together in a friendly manner, with Betty in front, bowling her hoop.

Elsie takes my arm as we turn up the path which leads over the moor, and says — quite untruthfully — that I have always been so kind to her. "Oh yes, you have, Mrs. Christie — I mean to say you don't try and make me feel small. Look at the other night — I'd have laughed at Mr. MacArbin if you hadn't stopped me. I thought he'd done it for a lark. I don't know much about *Scotch* people, you see."

I reply that I have suffered from the same disability myself, and a fellow feeling makes us wondrous kind.

"I knew you'd done it on purpose," she says triumphantly.

After walking on in silence for a minute or two, Elsie says the reason she wanted to see me was she wanted to ask me something important — don't I think a girl ought to be sure she really loves a man before she marries him? People do make mistakes sometimes, don't they? *She* likes a man with a bit of life about him — "a bit of sauce," says Miss Baker, pinching my arm confidentially. "*You* know the kind. There's a boy up at the Hotel, now — why he keeps the whole place in raws. I mean to say he's simply a scream. Now I dare say you thought I was a bit *dumb* — didn't you, Mrs. Christie? Well, I dare say I am, up at Burnside — Guthrie's so serious, and as for the old lady — well, I mean to say she's apt to put a wet blanket on any girl. The funny thing is," she continues, looking up at me very innocently out of her wide green eyes, "the funny thing is, it was just Guthrie being serious and different from the other boys that made me take to him — I was potty about him, you know — but I mean to say it would be too much of a good thing if you couldn't ever have a bit of fun."

I have never liked Elsie Baker so much as I do at this moment — I feel a strange affection towards her. She is being absolutely sincere with me — this is the real Elsie bereft of all her shams. There are tears in the green eyes.

I press her arm and tell her that Guthrie likes a bit of fun sometimes.

"Yes, but it's not *my* kind of fun," she replies earnestly. "And I don't understand it, and he doesn't understand *my* kind of fun. And I mean to say we wouldn't be happy together, I know we wouldn't," says the real Elsie, now weeping openly into a pale pink silk handkerchief, which fills the air with erotic perfume.

I squeeze her arm again — it is so difficult to know what to say, and I am so terrified of saying the wrong thing.

"You don't think I'm silly?" she asks.

"I think you are very wise," I reply comfortingly. "One of the most important things in married life is to understand each other's fun."

Elsie scrubs her eyes, and looks up at me earnestly. "I do hope you're happily married," she says.

I forgive the unpardonable sin, because she is ignorant of her transgression, and reply that I am. "Tim and I like the same kind of fun, we do the silliest things together —"

She squeezes my arm. "I do love you," she says, just as Betty might say it. We walk on in amicable silence.

"D'you think Guthrie will be awfully cut up?" she asks at last. This is dangerous ground; I search for some noncommittal reply, and murmur that he will get over it in time.

"Life *is* sad, isn't it?" she says with a sigh. "I mean to say you can't *help* hurting people, can you? You can't sacrifice yourself for another person — at least it wouldn't be any good, not if we weren't going to be happy."

"No good at all," I reply fervently.

"I'm glad you think it wouldn't be any good — I mean to say I do want you to see my side. I wish you could meet Stuart sometime," she continues, brightening a little. "You'd like Stuart, Mrs. Christie, I know you would. He'd have you in raws. Why, I'm quite sore to-day after the way he had me in raws last night. I mean to say I do like a good laugh, don't *you*? Oh dear, I wish you could see his take-offs; he's as good as a pantomime, he is really."

This description has a familiar sound, and I feel fairly certain that Elsie's new friend must be the gentleman who made such an impression upon Mrs. MacTurk. I enquire tactfully as to his identity and am confirmed in my suspicion.

"Yes, that's him," Elsie says. "Mr. Stuart Thompson — oh, he *is* a scream! He's taking Dad and I to Inverness this afternoon to see Charlie Lloyd in *I Take the Cake*. Have you ever seen it, Mrs. Christie?"

"It sounds very funny, but I thought you were coming to tea at Burnside."

"Oh, that's just it," Elsie says unblushingly. "You see it would be a bit awkward for me, wouldn't it? I mean *you* could tell Guthrie I'm not coming."

I suggest she should tell Guthrie herself, but Elsie says I could do it better. "You don't need to tell him where I've gone," she points out. "Just say I'm not coming, and that'll let him down gradually — I mean to say he'll soon find out about Stuart, and Guthrie isn't the kind to be a nuisance."

I realise at once that my companion has had some experience in being "off with the old love," but that her technique differs considerably from the advice of the adage. In fact, the strange creature uses the "new love" as a kind of boot-jack.

Betty is waiting for us on the crest of the hill. "How slow you walk!" she says. "This hoop's no good, I can't bowl it over the stones. I wish I had bought that ball, and then Annie and me could have played catches with it. D'you think if we went back now the girl would let me change it?"

I reply that I am quite sure she would *not*, and that we shall be late for lunch unless we hurry.

"Why aren't you hurrying then?" Betty says reproachfully. "Is Miss Baker coming to lunch with us?"

Miss Baker says she must go home to her father, and she is going to Inverness this afternoon to see a talkie. Upon which Betty exclaims rapturously, "Oh, how lovely! Can I come too? Is Guthrie going? Oh, do say I can come."

I entice my daughter away by all sorts of rash promises, and we wend our way homewards.

"You might have let me go," Betty points out. "She'd have *had* to take me if you said I could, whether she wanted to or not."

"But you wouldn't want to go unless she wanted you," I suggest, somewhat taken aback at this strange point of view.

"Of course I wanted to go," replies Betty firmly.

Lunch has begun, and Betty and I slip into our places, feeling rather guilty. Mrs. Loudon smiles encouragingly and asks if we have had a nice walk.

185

"It was lovely," says Betty. "I bought a hoop, but it wouldn't bowl properly over the stones, so now I wish I hadn't."

"I suppose it was the hoop that made you so late," suggests Guthrie teasingly.

"Oh no, it was because Mummie and Miss Baker walked so slow — Miss Baker was there, you know. She's going to Inverness this afternoon to see a talkie. I wish *we* could go to Inverness," says my irrepressible daughter, hopefully.

Guthrie looks rather puzzled. "But Miss Baker is coming here to tea."

"Oh no, she's not," replies Betty confidently. "She's going to Inverness — isn't she, Mummie?"

I had intended to give Guthrie the message in private, but perhaps this is the best way after all. At any rate he can ask for no details with the glare of the limelight upon him. Thus reflecting I confirm Betty's information.

Everyone looks surprised.

The advent of the postman turns the conversation into other channels. I open a letter from Bryan's headmaster and find that it contains the distressing news that my son has developed chicken-pox.

This disaster is received by my companions in various ways. Betty continues to absorb apple-tart quite undismayed by her brother's misfortune.

"Poor lad!" says Mrs. Loudon sympathetically. "How will he have got that, I wonder."

"Chicken-pox is nothing," Guthrie remarks comfortingly. "Just an excuse for a slack, and lots of fun in the san. I remember when I had chicken-pox we had the time of our young lives —"

"Chicken-pox!" exclaims Mrs. Falconer. "Us girls all had chicken-pox together in November 1900 — or it may have been 1901. I was quite grown up, and I remember being very distressed in case it should leave holes and spoil my appearance. It *must* have been in November, because I remember distinctly us looking out of the window with our spotty faces to see Papa and Edward letting off the fireworks in the garden for Guy Fawkes — or of course it *may* have been for the relief of Mafeking and not for Guy Fawkes at all. At any rate Alice caught a severe cold from being out of bed and not putting on her bedroom slippers. You remember what severe colds Alice used to get, Elspeth? Papa always said if you *breathed* too hard near Alice she got cold at once. That was just dear Papa's fun, of course, because a person breathing near you could not possibly give you cold. I always say if you tie a silk handkerchief round your head at night it prevents you from taking cold. Have you ever tried that, Elspeth? It is a remarkable preventative, but it *must* be silk, of course."

"I scarcely ever take cold," says Mrs. Loudon shortly.

"How fortunate you are!" exclaims her cousin. "Isn't she fortunate, Mrs. Christie? A cold in the head is such a disfiguring complaint, and nobody is the least sympathetic. I declare I would rather have appendicitis than a cold in the head."

"Bryan has colds too," says Betty suddenly. "Doesn't he, Mummie? And now he's got chicken-pox — what is chicken-pox like? Is it like a cold?"

"Chicken-pox is spots," declares Mrs. Falconer. She takes a deep breath, and is about to elaborate the theme, but Betty is too quick for her.

"I had spots at Kiltwinkle," she says breathlessly, "and Mummie thought it was measles, but the doctor said it was indirections of diet. Did you ever have indirections of diet, Guthrie?"

Guthrie says, "Frequently, after a heavy night at sea."

"It's horrid, isn't it? Bryan *never* has it, but then, of course, he's older than me. Sometimes he's five years older than me, and sometimes only four."

Guthrie asks in pardonable surprise how this thing can be, whereupon Betty explains kindly.

"Well, you see," she says, "he used to be eleven, when I was six, and then I had a birthday that made me seven, but Bryan's still only eleven, so he's only four years older than me now."

After a moment's thought Guthrie says that he sees.

All this has little bearing on poor Bryan's misfortune, but when we have finished lunch and are taking coffee on the veranda, Mrs. Loudon returns to the subject and makes sympathetic enquiries about his condition. I answer them from the meagre information contained in Mr. Parker's letter.

"Did you say he was at Nearhampton School?" cries Mrs. Falconer, pouncing suddenly on the name like a kitten on a ball of wool. "How very strange! That is where the Anstruthers' boy is at school — I always thought it such a funny name. You remember Frances Anstruther, Elspeth? This is her grandson, of course — such a charming boy — I saw him once when he was two years old, and he was very big for his age. I must really write to Frances and tell her about it. What a strange coincidence!"

Mrs. Loudon and I discuss the Anstruthers under cover of Mrs. Falconer's flow of talk. She is completely wound up, and seems quite oblivious of the fact that nobody is listening to her.

"I used to know Frances Anstruther well," Mrs. Loudon says. "We were real friends at one time, and then, quite suddenly, the pith seemed to go out of our friendship, and we drifted apart — perhaps you're too young to understand — and now if we meet it's just for the sake of what was, and to repeat, and to remember."

I tell her that I do understand, and that I know Mrs. Anstruther quite well — and am suddenly aghast at the lie. How do I know her? We have met quite frequently, it is true, and discussed the weather, and servants, and the merits and demerits of Nearhampton School. Well, this is one way of knowing a person, I suppose; to know the outline, not the detail; to sit on the veranda and look at the contour of the hill — that shoulder, such a jagged shoulder it looks, running down steeply into the silver water of the loch. I know Mrs. Anstruther in that way — just a few jags, sticking up into the blue sky, just a rounded piece of hill with a few pine-trees on it. Some day I may climb the hill and feel the smoothness of the jagged rocks, and find a piece of bog-myrtle in a crevice, or move a stone and see the ants and beetles wriggling amongst the pale roots of grass.

"Dreaming again, Hester?" says Mrs. Loudon, and I can see her smiling at me behind her glasses. "What a dreamer the girl is, to be sure."

"— but in those days," says Mrs. Falconer, evidently finishing a long and complicated story about her girlhood, "in those days nobody talked about being happy, like they do now — nobody minded whether children were happy, the really important thing was that they should be good. But I really think that people were just as happy as they are now, only they never thought about whether they were or not."

TUESDAY: 14TH JUNE

I VISIT INVERNESS WITH TONY, AND RESCUE A FAIRY PRINCESS

I receive a letter from Tim at breakfast time, saying that he will travel north on Thursday night, and arrive at Avielochan some time on Friday. This is thrilling news. Mrs. Loudon is delighted too, and says she knew the man would come, and she thinks we had better have another dinner-party for him, and ask the MacQuills this time, and perhaps the Farquhars from the Hall.

"I suppose you'll have no further use for *us* after Friday," Guthrie says, looking up from a plate piled with bacon, and running with tomato juice. "Once that husband of yours is here, we lesser mortals will have to take a back seat."

I reply primly that Tim and I are old married folk, and completely inured to each other's charms.

"Look at her, Mother — she's blushing," says the dreadful man with a grin.

"I'm not blushing," I retort indignantly. "My skin is so fair that when I eat tomatoes they show through."

"Tell me when you've quite finished girding at each other," says Mrs. Loudon with asperity. "There's some things I want fetched from Inverness, and dear knows how I'm to get them here. Dobbie says he wants a whole day at the car, the engine's knocking like a riveting machine, and he thinks it's a bludgeon pin or something."

Guthrie says he's sorry to hear about it, but he fails to see what he can do, unless his mother wants him to go to Inverness on Donald's push-bike. It's only a hundred-odd miles there and back, of course, but the bike is tied together with bootlaces — or perhaps she would like him to ride over on the fat pony which is used for mowing the lawn.

Mrs. Loudon retorts that she wants nothing except that he should have some sense, and he had better go and catch fish, as that's about all he's good for.

At this moment Tony arrives and says the Bentley wants exercising, and will I go for a run. Mrs. Loudon jumps at this chance of getting her shopping done, and asks shamelessly if the Bentley would run well in the direction of Inverness. Tony replies that it would like nothing better; we can go one way — by some place with an unpronounceable name — lunch at Inverness, and return the other way.

Mrs. Loudon says, "You really should see it, Hester."

Guthrie says, "Why should she? I can't think why anyone should want to."

Once it is known in the house that I am setting forth upon this expedition, I am besieged by people with commissions to be done. Mrs. Falconer wants some wool matched, and two pairs of black cashmere stockings; Mrs. Loudon has a long list of things — chiefly wine and groceries; Guthrie wants flies and four new casts; Annie requires elastic and buttons for Betty's underwear.

All this takes time, but at last we are ready to start. Tony says would I like to drive. I am amazed and touched at this proof of friendship, but refuse the offer unconditionally — the Bentley is so enormous compared with our small shabby Cassandra that I feel sure it would run away with me, and so disgrace me for ever in Tony's eyes.

Tony says, "Just as you like, of course," and steers carefully out of the gate. We float along rapidly amongst the mountains and the forests, enjoying the lovely breeze.

We have gone quite a long way — I don't know how far — and are rounding a very sharp bend with considerable care, when Tony swerves to the side of the road, and stops suddenly with a jarring of brakes.

"Good Lord!" he exclaims.

The cause of his consternation is at once apparent: a small yellow sports car is leaning drunkenly against a tree at the side of the road. One wheel is buckled and the windscreen is a mass of splinters.

"It's Hector MacQuill's car," Tony says anxiously. "The reckless devil has done it this time with a vengeance. I hope to goodness nobody's hurt. We'd better see —"

I begin getting out, but Tony seizes my arm. "You stay where you are, Hester," he says firmly.

At this moment Hector MacQuill appears from amongst the trees; he looks slightly dazed but appears to be unharmed.

193

"What's all this, Hector?" cries Tony in a relieved tone of voice. "You seem to have smashed up the Yellow Peril successfully — I knew you'd do it some day."

"I wish to goodness I had chosen some other day," replies the young man gloomily. "I don't care a blow about the car — the thing is we're in a frightful hole —"

"I can see that," Tony says facetiously.

"Perhaps I could speak to you for a minute," says Hector, with a glance at me.

Tony follows him over to the car, and they discuss something in low voices — I can't help wondering what it is all about. The car seems to be completely wrecked, and I see nothing for it but to go to the nearest garage, and send a break-down lorry.

After some minutes' conversation, Tony comes back to me, his eyes sparkling with mischief.

"You'll never guess what's happened," he says mysteriously. "Here's our friend Hector running off with Miss MacArbin. Who said Romance was dead?"

"Miss MacArbin!" I exclaim.

"None other," responds Tony. "He has a precedent for the deed, of course. I confess I did not think her wildly exciting, but there's no accounting for tastes. Perhaps the explanation lies in the fact that forbidden fruit is always the sweetest — anyway, here they are, and lucky to be alive — I don't know what happened. Hector is in such a state that he doesn't know himself."

"But where *is* Miss MacArbin?"

"Hiding in the trees and awaiting our decision," replies Tony dramatically. "Shall we bind them with the towing rope and deliver them to their respective families, or shall we drive on, and leave them to their fate, or shall we risk the wrath of both their clans, and further love's young dream by taking them to Inverness and putting them in the train? These are the three courses open to us, as far as I can see."

"But are they — do they —" I stammer.

"Apparently they are, and do," he replies gravely. "They have been meeting secretly for some time, and are quite convinced that they wish to follow the example of their notorious forbears."

"Well, I suppose they know their own minds —"

"I suppose nothing of the kind," says Tony with a twinkle in his eyes. "And it is quite against my principles to help anybody to marry anybody else. I am convinced that marriage is an overrated sport — except, of course, in exceptional cases. These two young people will probably live to curse our names — unless Hector succeeds in smashing himself up before the year is out. However, it's none of our business —"

"You *will* give us a lift, won't you, Mrs. Christie?" says Hector, himself, coming forward and putting an end to Tony's unseasonable dissertation. "We don't want to get anybody into trouble, but —"

"Of course we're going to help you!" I exclaim.

"I say, it's awfully good of you," he says, his brow clearing. "I'll just get hold of Deirdre and tell her the good news."

Tony is now busy unstrapping the suitcases from the back of the ill-fated Yellow Peril, and transferring them to the luggage-grid of the Bentley.

"It's rather fun, isn't it, Hester?" he says. "But we shall have to be careful not to get mixed up in it — there's going to be an unholy row when it's discovered."

Miss MacArbin now appears from her hiding-place looking more ethereal than ever, and I feel glad that the Fairy Princess has got a Prince worthy of her beauty. They make a splendid pair.

"You know Mrs. Christie, don't you, Deirdre?" says Hector, putting his arm through hers and gazing at her with adoring eyes.

"Of course I do," she replies.

"We met at the dinner-party, didn't we?"

"And once — nearly — before that," says Miss MacArbin with her sunlit smile. "I was the White Lady at Castle Darroch."

"And you thought she was the ghost of Seónaid," cries Hector boyishly. "By Jove, that was a near thing. I thought some of you saw me running into the wood when the rain came. Deirdre and I found the ruin a good place to meet — there is a secret passage from the tower which we found useful on more than one occasion."

"Well, jump in — if you've finished talking," Tony says. "And you had better cover yourselves with the rugs when we get near Inverness — Mrs. Christie and I don't want our throats cut by Clan MacQuill, nor our bodies thrown into Loch-an-Darroch by Clan MacArbin —"

"The whole thing is awful rot, isn't it?" says Hector, helping his fellow runaway into the car. "If Father could only *see* Deirdre —"

The Bentley's pace precludes any further conversation with our passengers. The miles flash by, and it seems but a few minutes before we are running through the streets of Inverness. By this time, however, Tony has outlined a plan which seems to me a feasible one. Deirdre and I are to be dropped at the entrance to the station, we are to take two tickets to Edinburgh, and make our way to the platform. Tony will park the car, and he and Hector will take two platform tickets and meet us at the train. Hector and I will then exchange tickets, and the runaways will get into different parts of the train. In this way the two victims of the feud will not be seen by anybody in each other's company — a circumstance which would at once give rise to talk and conjecture.

The plan is carried out without a hitch. Deirdre meets a friend on the way to the booking office, but, as her companion is merely an innocuous female, no suspicions are aroused. I find her a comfortable seat in the train and wish her the best of luck.

"I do hope we'll meet again," says Miss MacArbin.

"We must," I reply firmly.

She does not burden me with thanks, for which I feel suitably grateful.

"I'm rather frightened, Mrs. Christie," she says suddenly. "It's such a plunge — do you think they'll ever forgive us?"

"Of course they will — and even if they don't he's a perfect dear," I tell her comfortingly.

So I leave her and walk down the platform to meet the others. Tony is bubbling with mirth. "We've just

197

seen old Brown," he says. "The biggest gossip of the district — if only he knew what was afoot —"

Hector is grave, and I like him for it. "I shall never forget what you have done for us," he says as he shakes hands. "Once the train starts I shall go and find her. She'll be feeling rather scared, I expect."

We wish him every happiness, and leave him to his fate.

"Well," says Tony. "I don't know what you feel about it, but I'm simply starving — it's frightfully late."

We repair to a small hotel and order lunch. Tony is in splendid form, and full of amusing comments on our adventure. He is a most entertaining companion when he is in this mood.

By the time we have finished it is nearly tea-time. Tony says it is too much trouble to move, and he thinks we should stay where we are and order tea. The waiter, who has just brought the bill, looks somewhat surprised at Tony's remark, as we have both eaten enormously of veal-and-ham pie and various other substantial dishes. After a certain amount of byplay for the waiter's benefit, Tony is persuaded not to order tea at present, and I manage to drag him away.

The drive home is accomplished in record time.

"Not a word about to-day's doings to *anyone*, if you value your life," says Tony as we turn in at the gate, and I realise with a thrill of excitement that he is only half joking. This elopement is bound to cause a tremendous stir in the neighbourhood, and the consequences are wrapped in the mysterious veils of the future.

Mrs. Loudon has heard the approach of the car, and comes out to meet us, and, at the sight of my hostess, I suddenly remember that I have done none of the important commissions which were entrusted to me before starting. I have brought back from Inverness neither wine nor groceries, neither wool nor flies. What an awful thing! I would give five pounds — ill though I could spare it — if, with a wave of a magic wand, the car could be filled with the required number of parcels — but, alas, the days of miracles are past.

I look at Tony and Tony looks at me. I can see that he has just remembered too.

"Good Lord!" he exclaims. "We've done it this time."

Mrs. Loudon is surprised when she sees no parcels in the car, and even more astonished when I confess that I forgot all about the shopping.

"Oh well," she says. "I suppose we'll have to manage somehow — never mind about it. You enjoyed yourself, I suppose, and that's the main thing."

Mrs. Falconer is less forgiving; she treats me to a homily on the subject of memory, in which Papa comes out very strong. "Papa was very anxious that us girls should all have good memories," she says. "So he engaged a man to come and teach us the right way to remember things. This man had a system — quite infallible it was. Say you wanted to remember seventy-four, you had to think of seven apples and four bananas on a dessert dish. But one day when he was going away he forgot his umbrella, and Mama — who had never liked the man, he was very good-looking, of course — said that a man who forgot his umbrella was

199

not fit to teach anyone how to remember things. So that was the end of it, and we never learnt any more."

Guthrie says: "It's easy to remember things unless your mind is full of something else."

I have no idea what he means, as he can't possibly know anything about Hector and Deirdre MacArbin.

WEDNESDAY: 15TH JUNE

GUTHRIE AND I VISIT ELSIE

Awake with a feeling that something exciting has happened, and decide that it must be the result of yesterday's adventure. The breakfast-table is buzzing with the news of the elopement — brought to the house with the milk. I listen to it all in silence, and find great difficulty in concealing the fact that I know more about it than anyone else.

Guthrie says he didn't think either of them had so much spirit, to which Mrs. Loudon replies that those quiet people are always the worst — and anyway she hopes this will be the end of that ridiculous feud.

"It wasn't last time," says Guthrie. "I mean when old Hector went off with Seónaid, it made the feud worse than ever."

"My dear Guthrie, this is the twentieth century," replies his mother tartly.

"But is it?" Guthrie says, waving his hands in the effort to explain. "*We're* living in the twentieth century, of course, but are *they*?"

Mrs. Loudon's answer is a snort. She has no patience with ideas of this kind.

"Don't you see," says Guthrie, elaborating his theme with complete disregard of his mother's scornful attitude, "don't you see if you go on living in the same house — like the MacQuills — for hundreds of years, you are bound to develop at a slower rate than people who move about the world and see things with their eyes? Castle Quill was at its zenith in the sixteenth century, or thereabouts, and its atmosphere is thick with ghosts. Anybody living in Castle Quill is living in the sixteenth century."

"Perfect nonsense!" says Mrs. Loudon, rising from the table and collecting her letters. "And anyway that doesn't account for the MacArbins."

"Oh, the MacArbins!" says Guthrie, racking his brains for an answer to this. "The MacArbins take their sixteenth-century atmosphere with them wherever they go —"

We finish our breakfast in peace after Mrs. Loudon's departure, and Guthrie asks if I will walk over to the Hotel with him this morning to call on Elsie Baker, who has not been seen nor heard of for two days. I gather that Guthrie has written to her, and sent the letter over by the garden-boy, but that he has received no answer. All this does not surprise me in the least, as I realise that it is part of Elsie's plan to "let him down gradually."

"You had better go by yourself," I tell him, for I have no wish to be present at the interview. "I should only be in the way."

Guthrie is so downcast at my refusal, and so insistent that I shall accompany him, that, in the end, I am obliged to go.

"You see, I think the poor little thing must be ill, Hester," he says, as he opens the gate for me. "You could go up and see her in bed, couldn't you?"

I am pretty certain that Miss Baker is perfectly well, and, far from languishing in bed, has probably been touring the countryside in "Stuart's" car. Every step of the way I feel increasingly regretful that I have come, and send up silent prayers that Miss Baker may be out. I have no experience in delicate situations of this kind, and no wish to be involved in one.

"Poor little thing!" Guthrie continues, working himself up into a passion of pity for Elsie's imaginary sufferings. "I wonder who looks after her when she is ill — she has no mother, poor child! I can't bear to think of her lying there, day after day, with nobody to take care of her."

"Don't think of it, then," I reply lightly. "Wait and see whether she requires any pity before you waste it on her."

"You're awfully down on Elsie," he says reproachfully. "I never thought *you* could be so unsympathetic."

"I shall wait and see if any sympathy is needed."

"Poor little thing!" Guthrie continues. "She has never had a chance. Once we are married she will be able to stay with Mother while I am at sea —"

"You are most certainly at sea if you visualise Elsie Baker settling down with your mother at Holmgarth," I reply brutally.

"I thought you liked Elsie!" he exclaims.

"I do quite like her at times," I reply, with strict regard for the truth. "But your mother doesn't — and

203

Elsie doesn't like your mother. They would be bored to death with each other in two days. It means choosing between them, and the sooner you realise that the better."

"I have chosen," Guthrie replies sulkily.

This conversation has raised my spirits. I feel so annoyed with Guthrie for his obstinacy and stupidity that I don't care whether he gets hurt or not. Yes, you have chosen, and so has she, I think to myself, reflecting with cruel satisfaction that the coming interview — if interview there be — will give my self-satisfied young friend the shock of his life.

My prayers for Miss Baker's absence from home are not answered by an All-wise Providence. We find her stretched upon a deck-chair on the terrace in front of the Hotel reading a novel, and exposing quite a thrilling amount of very creditable leg, encased in Elephant Brand silk hose, at eight and eleven a pair.

"Elsie, have you been ill?" asks Guthrie anxiously. "No, don't go away, Hester."

"No, don't go away, Mrs. Christie," echoes Elsie. "Guthrie will bring another chair for you."

Can it be that she is slightly nervous? Perhaps she is not quite so experienced in matters of this kind as I imagined. I sit down, unwillingly enough, and ask what she has been doing with herself.

"Oh, we've been all over the place," says Elsie, with studied carelessness. "Mr. Stuart Thompson has been taking Dad and I for spins in his car."

Guthrie looks extremely taken aback at this news, but manages to control his feelings. "That was very

204

nice," he says. "But you could have gone for spins with me, if I'd known you wanted to. I thought you must be ill or something — did you get my letter?"

"Oh yes — but I really hadn't time to write — we've been ever so busy with one thing and another."

"Well, I'm glad you weren't ill," says Guthrie in a far-from-glad tone of voice. "What about this afternoon — would you like to come to tea, and fish afterwards?"

"I'm rather off fishing just now — I mean to say it's a bit slow. Besides, I've promised to go to Inverness this afternoon with Stuart," replies the lady candidly.

At this moment I see a large, fat shape — clad all in green — emerge from the Hotel, and realise that it is Mrs. MacTurk. For once she appears to me in the guise of an angel. I murmur that I simply *must* speak to her for a minute, and dash off, leaving the disillusioned lovers to their fate.

Mrs. MacTurk is delighted to see me, and welcomes me warmly. She evidently bears me no ill-will for her discomfiture on Sunday. (I had nothing to do with it, of course, but I feel that it is magnanimous of her to be so pleased to see me.) I ask breathlessly after all her relations, and am immediately involved — as I had hoped — in long descriptions of their various conditions. We stroll round the hotel garden in amicable conversation.

"I had no idea," says Mrs. MacTurk suddenly, "that Mrs. Loudon had a sister living with her —"

"Cousin," I murmur.

"Oh, it's a cousin, is it? Does she always talk like that?"

"Yes, always," I reply firmly.

"Dear me — it *must* be trying. Is the poor thing quite all right, Mrs. Christie?" asks Mrs. MacTurk with an upward movement of her brows.

"Oh, *quite* all right," I reply hurriedly.

"Well, well, she'll be quite harmless anyway, I suppose," says Mrs. MacTurk, evidently unconvinced by my assurance, "or Mrs. Loudon would scarcely risk having her about. You've seen no *dangerous signs*?"

"Oh, no."

"Still, there's no *knowing* with anybody like that," says the good lady anxiously. "They might go off suddenly, Mr. MacTurk says, and then where would you be? Such a strange way she had of talking — I declare it made me feel quite queer. I hope you lock your door at night, Mrs. Christie. I know I would. But anyway when I told Mr. MacTurk about it, and we had talked it over, we came to the conclusion that *it wouldn't do to have her here*."

"To have her here?" I repeat in amazement.

"To have her to dinner," explains Mrs. MacTurk. "People talk so in an hotel — you know the way they talk, Mrs. Christie — and Mr. MacTurk and I feel it wouldn't do — unless you could come without her, of course —" she adds hopefully.

"Oh, we couldn't possibly come without her," I reply firmly. "She would be so dreadfully hurt — but of course I quite understand your feelings —"

"It's very disappointing," she says sadly. "But Mr. MacTurk is very strong about it. It was lucky I said nothing about it to Mrs. Loudon. I shouldn't like her to be disappointed — and it seems a bit inhospitable somehow. You didn't mention it to her, did you?"

I comfort her as best I can, and assure her that Mrs. Loudon knows nothing of the projected dinner, and therefore will not be disappointed when it does not materialise.

"Well, that's one mercy," she says, more cheerfully. "I was afraid you might have said something."

Guthrie is waiting for us on our return; he seems dazed, and has to be reminded that he has the pleasure of Mrs. MacTurk's acquaintance.

"Oh yes, of course," he says. "How stupid of me! I don't know what I can have been thinking of."

I know exactly what he has been thinking of, but naturally refrain from saying so.

Presently Guthrie and I find ourselves walking home across the moor. He is very silent, and somewhat morose, and I can't help wondering what has happened — in other words has he definitely got the boot, or is he still in a state of suspense?

"Hester," says my companion suddenly, "I can't understand Elsie at all. I'm afraid this man she has been going about with has not a very good influence over her — you can't think how queer she was to-day."

I reply lightly that ladies have the privilege of changing their minds.

"You mean she has changed her mind about *me*?" he asks incredulously, and he looks so like a little boy who has offered somebody his cake and has had it thrown back in his face that I have to laugh.

"It looks a little like that," I gasp.

"But — but he's the most awful bounder — I *saw* the fellow — it's all very well for you to laugh at me, Hester, but he really is."

"I can well believe it," I reply, as soon as I can speak. "From the various accounts I have had of Mr. Stuart Thompson I had visualised a bounder of the most bounding proclivities — but, all the same, Elsie will be much happier with him than she would ever have been with you — and I'm not laughing at *you* so much as the queer way things turn out in this queer world."

"Well," he says, "you're not very sympathetic, I must say."

"You've already said that to me this morning," I reply. "And my answer is the same as it was last time — I keep my sympathy until it is needed. Elsie did not require my sympathy, and neither do you. Accept my congratulations instead."

"What *do* you mean?"

"You know perfectly well what I mean, Guthrie. It would have been the greatest mistake for you to marry Elsie. It would have resulted in misery for you both, and for Mrs. Loudon as well. Fortunately Elsie has realised that you are not the right man for her, and has been trying to convey the fact to your slightly obtuse intelligence."

"You are pretty scathing, aren't you?"

"I'm a perfect beast," I own cheerfully. "But it's all for your good, my dear. Buck up and look a little more cheerful. You know as well as I do that this is the best thing that could have happened."

"I can't understand it at all," he says in a bewildered manner.

THURSDAY: 16TH JUNE

WE LUNCH AT AVIELOCHAN HOTEL AND SPEND THE EVENING AT THE FAIR

Guthrie comes down just as Mrs. Loudon and I are finishing breakfast.

"I suppose you are remembering that you are going over to lunch with the MacKenzies at Inverquill," says Mrs. Loudon, with an eye on Guthrie's oldest and most disreputable trousers.

"Oh, I put it off," replies her son, helping himself to porridge and cream with a liberal hand. "I thought we'd fish here —"

"Well, you can't then," announces Mrs. Loudon firmly. "At least you can fish here, but there will be no lunch."

"No lunch!"

"No. Mary's away to Inverness for the day — I promised the creature a day in Inverness, and she's meeting her cousin, and going to the pictures."

"But what about you?" demands Guthrie, not unreasonably. "I suppose I can share your bread and cheese, or whatever you're having."

"We're lunching at the Hotel," replies Mrs. Loudon. "You need not look so surprised, both of you. I worked out the whole thing in bed last night, and it's all settled, so there's no more to be said. Hester will enjoy lunching at the Hotel; she must be tired of seeing nobody but her host and hostess day in and day out. It will be a change for her, anyway."

"Hester will hate it," replies Guthrie gloomily, and I can't help feeling that he is probably right. Difficult situations will probably arise from meeting the Bakers and the MacTurks, and the presence of Tony will not make things any easier.

"It's Hester's last day, too,' adds Guthrie.

"It'll be *your* last day," replies his mother tartly, "if you look at Hester like that when her husband's here. If you want to come over with us to the Hotel, you can, but you would be far better to go over to Inverquill, and fish with Ian."

"I believe I would," agrees the wretched man. I really feel very sorry for him, and when Mrs. Loudon has departed, jingling her housekeeping keys, I beseech him to go to Inverquill, or Timbuctoo, or, in fact, anywhere except the Avielochan Hotel.

"Oh, I'll go to Inverquill," he says in martyr-like tones. "Ian will be quite glad; he said I could leave it open, but I thought we could have a nice long day on the loch. You can tell Mother I've gone."

It seems strange that I should always be saddled with messages which people don't want to deliver themselves. I try to believe that it is because my nature is sympathetic, but have an uncomfortable suspicion that it is because I am too weak-minded to refuse the job.

The morning flies past with incredible speed, and it is not until we are ready to start that I find an opportunity to give Mrs. Loudon the information.

"It's just as well," she says, in a relieved voice. "I'd never have thought of the Hotel with Guthrie. We would have had that goggle-eyed Baker girl tacked on to us the whole time. Where's Millie? It's time we were away."

We walk slowly over the moor. Mrs. Falconer's legs are less active than her tongue. She stops every few minutes to admire the view, and to inform us what Papa would have said if he had been here. Thus delayed, it is after one o'clock when we reach the Hotel, and most of the visitors have gone in to lunch.

"We'll have cocktails first," announces Mrs. Loudon surprisingly. "I've never tasted the things, and I've often wondered what like they were."

"You'll do as you please, of course, Elspeth," says Mrs. Falconer, sinking into a cane chair with a groan of fatigue. "I, for one, shall not risk it."

"You'll take sherry, then," says Mrs. Loudon firmly. "It will do you good." She summons the waiter in her queenliest manner, and orders two cocktails and one sherry.

"Yes, madame." He bows, and reels off a string of the different kinds obtainable at the Hotel. The list is long enough and peculiar enough to daunt a stout-hearted man, but Mrs. Loudon rises to the occasion nobly.

"I'll have a Broncho," she says gravely. "What about you, Hester? Two Bronchos, please. I don't know why you are laughing, Hester, but if it is a good joke you might share it with us. Good gracious, there's the Baker man!"

"The baker-man!" echoes Mrs. Falconer, peering round shortsightedly.

Mrs. Loudon is not listening. "He hasn't seen us," she announces in a relieved voice. Personally I feel sure Mr. Baker has seen us, but, not having sufficient aplomb to deal with the situation created by his Elsie, has shirked the issue by pretending to be stone blind.

We drink our cocktails peacefully, and enter the dining-room, where Mrs. Loudon's manner procures us the instant attention of the head waiter and a delightful table near the window. I look round and find to my satisfaction that all our neighbours are complete strangers. The MacTurks are at the other end of the room near the band, and the Bakers are giving a luncheon-party to their friends at the large centre table. Elsie is looking very pretty in flowered *voile*; she talks and laughs in an animated way, and seems to be enjoying herself immensely. The young man on her right with the fair wavy hair and the Adam's apple must be Guthrie's supplanter. She is so enchanted with his wit that it is not until the luncheon-party is nearly over that her eye falls upon me.

I should like to have to record that she turns pale, and that the laughter dies on her lips, but nothing of the sort occurs. She merely looks a trifle surprised, and smiles at me in a friendly manner.

Meanwhile Mrs. Loudon has seen Elsie and her *entourage*. She gives no sign of recognition, but her mouth hardens and her thin fingers pluck at her bread.

213

"We'll go when you've finished, Millie," she says quietly.

"But we haven't had the ice!" exclaims Mrs. Falconer, who enjoys her food. "Don't you want the ice, Elspeth?"

At this moment Tony appears through the swing doors. He sees us at once, and comes across the room to our table.

"Well," he says, smiling gravely. "This is an unexpected pleasure. Has Burnside been burnt to the ground or what?"

"What," I reply instantly.

"Ah, I'm glad it's what," he says. "Burnside is too pleasant a place to go up in smoke. May I sit down at your table? — and how does the Cannibal Feast strike you, Mrs. Loudon?"

"I don't understand it," replies Mrs. Loudon, moving her gloves and bag from the chair to make room for Tony.

"It's difficult, isn't it? Why should a Cannibal Queen fall for an Adam's apple? And the answer is because however tired an elephant may be, he can't sit down on his trunk."

"I'm afraid I don't follow you," says Mrs. Falconer helplessly.

"I like you all the better for it," replies Tony. "I simply can't bear being followed. If you knew what I had been through before the Adam's apple appeared on the scene and took the Hotel by storm, you would understand my feelings."

214

Mrs. Falconer gives up the unequal struggle, and falls to with a will upon the large pink ice which has appeared before her as if by magic. She is obviously afraid that "Elspeth" will drag her away before she has finished it.

The MacTurks now descend upon us, and invite us to take coffee in the lounge — an invitation which can hardly be refused without rank discourtesy. They wait politely until Mrs. Falconer's ice has disappeared, and then we all file into the lounge. Tony and I are the last through the swing-door. He holds it open for me, and whispers, "It's frightfully amusing, but I really don't know why."

Seats are found for us beneath the spreading branches of a palm tree, and Mr. MacTurk orders large cups of "special coffee" for the whole party. He induces Mrs. Loudon to try a Benedictine, and my poor friend is so bewildered at finding herself in this galley that she has not the strength to refuse. Mrs. MacTurk has seated herself as far away from Mrs. Falconer as possible, and keeps a wary eye on that harmless lady in case she should "go off suddenly."

"I suppose you've heard about the elopement," says Mr. MacTurk, turning to me with a beaming smile.

"It's the talk of the Hotel," adds Mrs. MacTurk. "I must say we've been lucky in our visit to Avielochan this year. It makes a difference if you've got something to talk about when you're in an hotel like this. It makes it so much more exciting on account of the feud — it's a real Highland feud, you know, Mrs. Christie."

"Yes, I know," I reply feebly.

215

"Mr. MacArbin was here last night — or no, it was the night before — looking for his sister. It was quite exciting. And then who should walk in but Sir Hector MacQuill, looking for his son —"

(I look at Tony for confirmation of this, and he nods imperceptibly, and whispers, "Frightful, wasn't it?")

"And we've made such a lot of nice friends this time," says Mr. MacTurk, continuing the saga.

"Indeed we have," agrees Mrs. MacTurk. "Mr. MacTurk and I were just saying this morning what a lot of nice friends we had made. Mrs. Loudon and Major Morley — and Captain Loudon, of course — and the Bakers, and Mr. Stuart Thompson. Everybody is sure that they're going to be married — I mean Elsie and Mr. Thompson — quite a romance it's been. I declare it's just like a book —"

Mrs. Loudon looks at me in a dazed manner. Her misery is apparent, and I wish that I could get her away and explain everything to her; but we can't do these obvious things in civilised society; we must sit still and smile at the right moment, and sip our "special coffee" until the correct time for departure arrives.

If it were not for Mrs. Loudon's misery I should be enjoying myself, for it is a pleasant party, and the MacTurks are on their best behaviour. I realise that it is only because they have accomplished their object, and that they have used me in a shameless manner as a means of getting to know Mrs. Loudon; but they are so kind and hospitable, and are trying so hard to be nice that I can't help liking them. I can hardly believe that these are the same people who were so rude to us at Kiltwinkle — so snobbish and vulgar and selfish.

The Baker party now bursts into the lounge, laughing and talking with gay abandon. Mr. Stuart Thompson is giving one of his famous "take-offs," to the intense amusement of his friends. Some of them are doubled up with mirth, others have the strength to beat him warmly on the back. They have evidently partaken of an excellent lunch at Mr. Baker's expense, and the champagne has been poured forth like water.

"Mr. Thompson is impersonating the manager," Tony whispers. "It is always the manager when he walks with his chest well forward like that. I believe his 'take-off' of me is very lifelike, and chiefly consists of remarking, in a strange high-pitched voice, 'Haw haw — don'tcherknow.' Have you ever heard me say, 'Haw haw — don'tcherknow,' Hester?"

I reply that it is a well-known fact that majors in His Majesty's Army are in the habit of saying, "Haw haw — don'tcherknow" at every opportunity.

"Well, you ought to know what you're talking about," says Tony, with a sigh. "The remark seems somewhat fatuous to me, I must say."

"Now don't you worry about what Mr. Thompson says," Mrs. MacTurk adjures him, bending towards him with a fat smile creasing her face. "It's just his fun, and he doesn't mean anything nasty. Why, he took off Mr. MacTurk the other day, and Mr. MacTurk didn't mind a bit —"

She breaks off, and looks up in time to see Mr. Baker come through the swing-door. He has been left behind

— obviously to tip the waiter and sign the bill. He stands there alone, looking for his guests, but his guests have vanished. They have no use for Mr. Baker except to foot the bill, and the little man is aware of the fact. He is a lonely, dejected figure and I can't help feeling sorry for him. Does he approve of Elsie's change of heart, I wonder; has he offered Mr. Thompson a partnership in that comfortable little business at Portsmouth; or does he realise that a man so inimitable at "take-offs" might make but a poor partner in a serious concern?

Mr. MacTurk, who has quite a kind heart, calls to Mr. Baker and invites him to join us, but the little man is too frightened to accept. He bows politely to the whole party — with a special obeisance to Mrs. Loudon — and trails away after his daughter and her friends.

"What's the matter, Hester?" enquires Tony. "Are you breaking your heart over Mr. Baker?"

"I am rather," I admit. "They are so horrid to him, and he's really rather a dear."

"You're too soft-hearted," Tony says. "He'll be as happy as a grig — whatever that may be — when the grandchildren begin to arrive. I can imagine Mr. Baker with a grandchild on either knee, jigging them up and down, and singing 'The fox is off to its den — oh.'"

I can imagine it too, and the vision is comforting. Tony is an astounding person.

At the correct moment Mrs. Loudon rises, and we say good-bye and are whirled home to Burnside in the Bentley. Mrs. Falconer is delighted with her "ride," and confesses that she never was a great walker, and, even when she was young, preferred to go in the carriage with Mama than to walk with the other girls. "But we always took it in turns," she adds with a sigh. "And there were so many of us that my turn did not come round as often as I could have wished." I commiserate with her — somewhat half-heartedly I fear. "Yes," she continues, "dear Mama liked to take us girls to pay calls with her — only one at a time, of course. She considered it an important part of our education to know exactly how many cards to leave at each house, and to learn to take part in cultured conversation."

Mrs. Loudon follows me into my room when I go to take off my hat, and I am not at all surprised, for I know she has been boiling with bewilderment and wrath for the last hour.

"Well!" she says, sitting down on my bed and looking at me. "Well, of all the blatant hussies! Guthrie will have to be told — it's beyond everything —"

"Guthrie knows," I tell her briefly. "I'd have told you before, but I didn't want to say anything until it was absolutely settled —"

"Guthrie knows that she's carrying on with that frightful-looking man?"

"She told him yesterday — at least she tried to tell him — Guthrie found it hard to believe —"

"Then it's off," she says. "Thank God the boy has come to his senses — and thank *you*, Hester. For I believe you had a lot to do with it, and I'll never forget it as long as I live — *Hester*."

She holds out her arms and I hug her tight. I try to tell her the truth of the matter, and point out that it was none of my doing, but simply because Elsie had the sense to see that Guthrie and she were unsuited to each other, but Mrs. Loudon does not listen. She is convinced that I — aided and abetted by that nice Major Morley — have saved her son from the clutches of a harpy. "I'll never forget it as long as I live," she says again. "If ever there's anything I can do for you — but there won't be — there never is, when you want there to be. There's the gong for tea, I declare. Come away, and get something to eat — I don't believe I ate much lunch, it seemed to choke me. Anyway, I'm starving now."

We go down to tea, arm in arm.

At tea Mrs. Loudon is as gay as a girl; she teases Mrs. Falconer, and crosses swords with Guthrie and me. But I notice that sometimes she looks at Guthrie when his attention is directed elsewhere, and there is a radiance in her face that is wonderful to see. She loves him so dearly. Her dry manner covers a very tender heart.

Guthrie has come back to her, and it is almost as if he had come back to her from the grave.

Dinner is over. We are all comfortably settled in the drawing-room, and Guthrie and I have started our usual game of chess. Guthrie is an extremely careful player, and ponders long over every move; he considers me rash to the verge of insanity, but has only managed to beat me once, so far. I will admit to the sacred page of my journal — though never to Guthrie — that my dashing moves are more often matters of pure luck than well-thought-out manœuvres.

"There's a car coming up the drive," says Mrs. Loudon suddenly.

"Can it be Tim?" I cry. It would be just like Tim to arrive before he was expected. Nothing pleases him more than to surprise people like that.

But our visitor is not Tim, it is Tony Morley. He comes in, smiling cheerfully, and is warmly welcomed by Mrs. Loudon. I notice that Mrs. Falconer and Guthrie greet him with perceptibly less warmth — he is no favourite with either of them.

"I wondered if any of you would like to come up to the fair," says Tony. "It's such a lovely mild night. There's a fair over at Inverquill — quite a good fair, with roundabouts and things. I could run you over in the car."

"What an extraordinary idea!" remarks Guthrie (moving his queen without having considered the matter with his usual care).

Tony is in no way dashed. "I thought Hester might like to see a real Highland fair," he says persuasively.

"So I should," I reply (taking Guthrie's queen with my last remaining knight, who has been lying in wait for her for some time). "I should simply love to see a real Highland fair."

"There's no real Highland about it," Guthrie says, pushing the board away crossly. "All fairs are exactly the same wherever they are — sordid shows with a crowd of dirty people shoving their elbows into your ribs —"

"Well, there's no need for you to go," says Mrs. Loudon. "Hester can go with Major Morley. I'd go myself if I were ten years younger, but it's not for an old woman like me to go gallivanting off to fairs at this time of night."

"Oh, if Hester wants to go, I'll go too," says Guthrie quickly. "I don't suppose she'll enjoy it when she gets there —"

I rush upstairs to change into warm clothes — tweeds will probably be best, and my thick grey coat with the fur collar, and a red tammy. I reflect, as I hastily powder my nose, that the evening will not be without its difficulties. Guthrie will take every opportunity of being rude to Tony (he is already in an unpleasant frame of mind) and Tony will retaliate by making a fool of Guthrie, which seems to give him untold pleasure. Why can't they be friendly and pleasant, as they were that dreadful morning when Betty was lost? How difficult life is! Difficult enough without people going out of their way to make things awkward for themselves and all around them.

For a moment I wish that I had refused to go, and then I look out of the window, and the night calls me. The sun is setting now, and, above the hills, the sky is aflame. It will soon be dark — and darkness is ideal for a fair. The lights flare so gaily in the darkness and throw dancing shadows on the jostling throngs. It will be fun. My spirits rise with a bound, and I feel ready to cope with anything.

Betty calls to me from her room, next door. "I can't sleep, Mummie," she says. "The sun's so glowing bright. It's making my room all red." There is a patter of bare feet, and Betty stands beside me. "You'll get cold," I point out, but only half-heartedly, for it seems impossible that anybody could get cold to-night. "No I won't," says Betty. "You can't get cold when it's quite warm." She kneels up on the window seat, and the setting sun turns her yellow curls to gold. "Mummie," she says thoughtfully. "Where is the sun's nest? I think it's just behind Ben Seoch, don't you? I think it's going there now, very slowly, because it's tired. I'd like to peep over Ben Seoch and see the sun settling down all warm and cosy in its nest —"

I pick up my daughter and carry her back to bed. "You settle down warm and cosy in *your* nest," I tell her, as I tuck her in. "I'll tell you about the sun to-morrow."

"Darling Mummie," she says sleepily. "Daddy's coming soon. How lovely that will be —"

My two cavaliers are waiting for me in the hall. They are a handsome enough pair to look at, for both are tall, and Guthrie is broad in proportion, but handsome is as handsome does, and it remains to be seen how they will behave themselves this evening. We climb into the Bentley and are off like the wind; it is a lovely sensation flying through the gloaming. All the light seems to have drained out of the woods, leaving them black as pitch; but, on the road, and over the open moor, there is still a ghostly sort of radiance, and the sky is not yet dark, but darkening fast. The Bentley makes short work of the twenty miles or so which stretch before us to Inverquill, and soon we hear the distant sound of the organ in the roundabout, and see the lights from the booths flaring in the twilight.

First we visit the shooting-gallery (in spite of Guthrie's repeated assurances that the coco-nut shies are infinitely more amusing). It is situated in a wooden shed, full of flaring light and a strange smell of humanity.

"Three shots a penny," yells a small man in an ancient khaki jacket which, I feel sure, saw its best days during the war. "Three shots a penny; only a penny for three shots, and win a brooch for your young lady, if you get 'em all bulls — come along, gentlemen, three shots a penny and win a brooch — make way there for the gentleman —"

A burly farmer hands his rifle to Tony with a wink. "If you would be aiming high left every time you might be getting a bull," he says confidentially. "For my part I'm better with a gun than one of these toys."

Tony thanks him and takes careful aim. At first his shots go rather wide, but after several pennies' worth, he settles down to it and gets three bulls without apparent difficulty. The khaki man congratulates him warmly upon his achievement, and invites him to take his pick of the brooches on the tray.

"I hope they are real," Tony says gravely. This is considered a splendid joke by the khaki man — and indeed by all who hear it.

"Oh, they're real enough," he says, winking slily. "This is Bond Street, this is. You won't find no sham julry on *my* tray."

224

Tony chooses one with two gold hearts transfixed by an arrow, and hands it to me with great solemnity.

By this time Guthrie has had enough of it — he has been shooting farther down the gallery — he returns to us, and says it is just as he thought, the rifles are all doctored, and the whole thing is an absolute fraud. I conclude that he has not been so successful as Tony in his shooting. He eyes my brooch — which I have pinned on to my coat — with scorn and disgust (it might be a black-beetle from the way he looks at it), and suggests that we should have a go at the coco-nut shies.

I feel that it is Guthrie's turn for a little consideration now, so we make our way in that direction. Here Guthrie displays tremendous prowess, and sends coco-nuts flying in all directions, much to the disgust of the coco-nut man and to the delight of all the onlookers. Tony and I are completely outclassed at this sport, but we share in his reflected glory, and back him up loyally in his argument with the owner of the stall, who tries to do him out of his hardly earned spoils. We leave the place in triumph, Guthrie carrying four large coco-nuts which are a perfect nuisance to him for the rest of the evening.

So far we have seen nothing the least different from any other fair. In fact most of the people in the booths have undoubtedly come from south of the Tweed. Guthrie points this out to Tony in a somewhat sarcastic tone of voice. Tony replies that we are only just starting, and the night is yet young. He seizes hold of a hurrying man, and asks what that crowd is "over there."

"If you're quick you'll see Jock Sprott," replies the man. "He's at it now."

"And what is he at?" asks Tony in dulcet tones.

The man glares at him indignantly. "Have ye never seen Jock Sprott throwing the hammer?" he enquires, and is gone before his rhetorical question can be answered.

"Come on, we *must* see Jock Sprott," Tony says, dragging us along at a tremendous pace. "Here's your chance to see something really Highland at last."

I demand breathlessly who he is, and why he throws hammers about.

"Oh, he's a Scotch relation of the man who could eat no fat," replies Tony glibly, "and he throws hammers about for a living — it's quite different from throwing them into the corner because they have hit you on the thumb when you were trying to knock in a nail."

We push through the crowd and arrive just in time to see the contest. A huge hammer is lying on the ground — it is the sort of hammer that a giant in a fairy-tale might be proud to own. It is such an enormous hammer that to me it does not look like a hammer at all.

Jock Sprott now appears from a small tent — Tony whispers that he has been in there, eating beef-steaks to make him strong, but I don't believe all Tony says. He is a huge Highlander in a kilt. He strides up to the hammer, spits on his hands, and takes the shaft in a firm grip — a whisper like the sound of rustling trees goes through the crowd. The moment has come; he lifts the hammer (his muscles bulging beneath his cotton shirt) and twirls round and round, and at every twirl the hammer rises higher and higher in the air. At last, when it is level with his outstretched arms, he lets go of it and away it goes down the field . . .

The throw is evidently a good one, for the crowd applauds loudly, and two solemn-faced umpires appear with tape measures, and discuss its merits. Jock seems to have a number of staunch backers in the crowd, and these push forward and question the umpires' decision, and make themselves disagreeable in various ways.

We watch several other broad and hefty men trying their skill and strength with the hammer, but they have not the same air of confidence as Jock, and have therefore fewer admirers and nobody to tackle the umpires on their behalf. Jock Sprott is proclaimed the victor amidst loud applause.

Guthrie says this is poor sport compared with tossing the caber, but, of course, we shan't see them tossing the caber at a rotten little fair like *this*.

We are pushing our way out of the crowd when suddenly we are confronted by a tall man in Highland dress — it is MacArbin. My first instinct is flight, and I believe that Tony feels the same almost overpowering impulse; but Guthrie — who, of course, has no reason to avoid him — presses forward and shakes him by the hand, and we are involved in talk with the unhappy man. I am quite shocked at the difference in him, which, I suppose, is due to distress over his sister's elopement. He seems years older, and his glossy self-confidence has completely gone.

227

"Have you heard from your sister, sir?" asks Guthrie, rushing in where angels might fear to tread.

"I have no sister," he replies — not dramatically, but just as if he were stating a sad fact. "No sister," he repeats, and, bowing to us with something of his old-time grace, he passes from us and is lost in the crowd.

"Good Lord!" Guthrie says. "I seem to have put my foot in it with the old chap. Who would have thought he would have taken Deirdre's marriage so much to heart? Hector's one of the best fellows going — I suppose he's still chewing away at his silly old feud."

Tony and I say nothing — perhaps he is as shocked as I am at the change in the proud Highlander — at any rate he lets Guthrie's tactlessness pass without comment, which shows that he is not feeling quite his usual self.

The roundabout is encompassed by a crowd of gaping children, the horses prance gaily in their red and gold trappings, and the organ blares forth a pot-pourri of popular tunes. All around is the darkness of the night and the silent hills, but here there is light and gaiety and noise.

"In eleven more months and ten more days I'll be out of the calaboose," shouts Tony, elbowing his way through the crowd. He has suddenly gone quite crazy, and his mood is infectious. I feel on for anything that's going, and squeeze after him through the lane he has made. We have lost Guthrie by this time, but perhaps it is just as well — I have already decided that it is a frightful mistake to come to a fair with two swains in attendance.

We mount two fiery-looking steeds and prance round and round — I have no idea how many turns we have. The flaring lights, the rhythm of the organ, and the hot happy faces of the riders melt into a sort of blur. Just in front of us is a fat woman who screams delightedly and waves to various friends in the crowd of watchers. Behind us a farm boy and his sweetheart hold hands and smile at each other in excited bliss. Tony's eyes are shining with a strange light, he has lost his hat, and his fair hair is standing on end. I can't believe that this is really the reserved and cynical Tony Morley. Surely there is some madness abroad in the June night that has got into his blood!

At last we decide that we have had enough, and climb down. I can hardly stand, and cling to Tony's solid arm like a drowning man.

"Giddy?" he enquires, looking down at me with smiling eyes. "I'm a bit giddy myself — feel as if I wanted to do something silly. Look here, Hester, I've got a grand idea — let's treat all these kids to a ride — shall we?"

I realise afresh how lovely it must be to be rich, and nod my head emphatically.

The owner of the roundabout — who is of a suitable build for his profession and possesses a shining red face — is delighted with Tony's offer, and agrees that ten shillings will give all the children a good ride. He therefore climbs on to a convenient tub and announces through a megaphone that a kind gentleman is giving a

229

free ride to all the children present. "Come along all of ye," he shouts. "Walk up, children — free ride for hevery one of ye."

For about half a minute nobody moves. The children are utterly incredulous of their good fortune . . . and then there is an absolute stampede. We are almost swept off our feet by the rush, and the roundabout man only saves himself from disaster by jumping nimbly off the tub and clutching Tony's arm.

"We've done it now, sir," he says, looking at the juvenile avalanche in dismay. "There'll be murder done — and 'ow on earth 'ull I ever get them children off those 'orses again?"

Tony evidently shares the fat man's views. He presses a pound note into the grubby hand and drags me away.

"For God's sake let's get out of this, Hester," he says. "I had no idea we were going to let Bedlam loose in the place."

Bedlam is loose indeed. The children have stormed the roundabout, and are fighting like demons over the horses. The air is rent with the battle cries of the victorious, and the shrieks of the fallen. A few fond parents are pushing through the throng and calling wildly for their young.

We fly from the scene, hand in hand, pursued by the noise and the commotion — from afar we hear the fat man shouting through his megaphone in despairing tones, and beseeching his young patrons to refrain from dragging each other off the horses and hitting each other on the nose.

"You'll *hall* get a free ride if you comes quiet," he bellows. "Hevery one of ye — stop it now, do. 'Ow can I start the 'orses if ye keeps on fighting?"

The booths are almost deserted, everyone having been drawn to the roundabout by the noise. Tony and I have ample leisure to stroll round and make our purchases. The booths are lighted with flares, as all booths should be; there is something mysterious and exciting about flares. The wind plays with them, blowing them this way and that, so that they almost vanish, and then leap up with renewed energy. The shadows dance and waver on the eager faces of the stall-holders as they bend forward over their wares; so that at one moment a man's face seems all nose, with two dark caverns below his temples for eyes, and the next moment he seems quite an ordinary little man with nothing remarkable about him. Two girls lean together, whispering, and the dancing red light makes them beautiful and hideous by turns. One of them laughs, throwing up her head, and her hair is like a red nimbus round her pallid face. I catch Tony's arm and tell him to look.

"It's queer, isn't it?" he says. "They live in their own world, just as important to them as ours is to us. We have never seen them before, and we shall never see them again, but to-night, just for a moment, our two worlds touch."

"Let's speak to them."

"No, it would spoil it," says Tony. "It's perfect as it is, and they probably drop their aitches — I wish I could paint."

I feel it would not matter if they dropped their aitches, it is the girls that interest me, not so much the picture they make. How do they live? What are they talking about? But at the same time I realise that they couldn't tell me what I want to know, even if they would; so we leave them and stroll on.

"I want a gingerbread-man," Tony says suddenly. "I simply must buy a gingerbread-man. Do you mean to tell me you haven't got a gingerbread-man?" he says to the girl at the sweet stall. "With gilt on the outside that you can lick off — no? Hester, I'm sorry, this isn't a real fair at all. They haven't got a gingerbread-man."

The girl is quite frightened and offers him a gingerbread-horse, but it has no gilt on it and Tony looks at it with scorn.

"How can we go on saying '*That* has taken the gilt off the gingerbread' if there never was any gilt on it?" he demands. "You see my point, don't you? Unless, of course, this horse was covered with gilt, and someone has licked it off already —"

The girl indignantly repudiates the suggestion.

"Oh well!" says Tony sadly. "Another illusion gone west . . ."

At the toy stall I buy a doll for Betty, and Tony buys her a monkey on a stick. I also invest in fairings for Mrs. Loudon, Mrs. Falconer and Annie. Tony shows me a small india-rubber frog — green, with goggling yellow eyes — and says he is going to give it to "our dear Guthrie" and don't I think it is a speaking likeness. I reply quite frankly that I can't see the smallest resemblance, which damps Tony's spirits for about twenty seconds.

We are passing a tent, covered with mystic signs and black cats, when the flap is suddenly thrown back, and a tall burly figure emerges from the gloom. It is the long-lost Guthrie, and he looks somewhat sheepish when he sees us.

"I've been looking everywhere for you," he announces.

"Have you really?" says Tony kindly. "What bad luck! But you'll know another time not to look for us in the fortune-teller's mystic abode. Hester and I make a point of never having our fortunes told."

"You probably do something far sillier," replies Guthrie, guessing right for once. The effect of his pronouncement is marred by the wretched coco-nuts, which escape from his clutches and roll in all directions. We collect three of them with some difficulty, owing to the darkness, but the fourth has gone forever.

"Never mind," Guthrie says. "Three is enough to make all the birds at Burnside thoroughly ill."

I feel we have been rather neglectful of Guthrie, so I enquire in my friendliest manner what the fortune-teller said to him. He responds at once to slight encouragement, and replies:

"Oh, just the usual rot. I am going a long journey over the sea, and I must beware of a girl with golden hair; and a brunette is going to save me from danger, and alter my whole life — what *is* a brunette?" asks Guthrie.

"Hester is," says Tony wickedly. "By the way, Loudon, the sybil didn't tell you that a tall man with a kind face was going to give you a frog, did she? Well, I don't think much of her then," and so saying he takes the frog out of his pocket and presents it to Guthrie with a low bow.

Guthrie looks at it with suspicion. He cannot make up his mind whether it is some new and deadly insult, or whether it is merely a joke.

"What on earth is *this* for?" he asks.

"For your bath," says Tony gravely. "And to remind you of me when we are far apart and the seas divide us."

"I think I had better give it to Betty," Guthrie says. "When I'm in my bath there's not much room for frogs."

I feel relieved and pleased at the way in which Guthrie has taken the joke, and congratulate myself upon the fact that they have actually spoken to each other without being rude.

"There seems to be the devil of a row going on at the roundabout," Guthrie says suddenly. "Let's push on, and see what's happening."

Tony and I refuse firmly, with one accord, to go near the place.

"It looks like a free fight," Guthrie continues, turning round and gazing at the roundabout with interest and animation. "Let's go over and have a look at it. We needn't get mixed up in it if Hester is nervous."

"It's nothing, absolutely nothing," Tony assures him. "They always go on like that at roundabouts."

234

"Rot," says Guthrie. "There's a row on, and I'm going over to see what it's about — you needn't come if you're frightened."

"I'm simply terrified," Tony replies. "But I'll try to be brave if Hester will stay with me, and hold my hand. Give my love to the roundabout man," he calls out to Guthrie's retreating back, "and meet us at the car if you get out of it alive."

The whole place is now beginning to close down. At some of the booths the flares have been extinguished, and the occupants are busy packing up their wares and taking down their tents and wooden stalls. Huge vans have appeared upon the scene, and men in shirt sleeves are busily engaged in packing them. We accost a small dirty youth and ask him if the fair is moving.

"We'll be on the road in twa hours," he replies briefly.

"What a life!" ejaculates Tony.

"Aye, it's a fine life," echoes the boy. "Ye get seeing the wurrld in a fair."

All mystery has departed from the fortune-teller's tent; it is merely a heap of dirty canvas. A large, fat woman with greasy black hair, and a red shawl pinned across her inadequately clad bosom, is dancing about with a flaming torch in her hand, directing operations in a shrill shrewish voice.

"Guthrie's sybil!" says Tony sadly. "I'm afraid we've stayed too long at the party."

"I think it is rather fun," I reply. "I like seeing things that I'm not meant to see — besides, it's not really very late."

"Mother said I was to be home at six to have my hair washed," says Tony in an absurd treble.

I tell him he's a perfect idiot and we walk on laughing.

"Here you are!" exclaims Guthrie, pouncing on us suddenly — so suddenly that we both nearly jump out of our skins. "Look here, you simply must come over and see the fun — people are knocking each other down — there's a funny little fat man with a megaphone — I want to get hold of him and find out all about it."

"I'm sure he knows nothing," says Tony untruthfully, "and if he did he wouldn't tell you. We're going home now, Hester's tired."

"But surely you can wait ten minutes."

"Not one minute. Do come on, Loudon. The show is all over now; Hester wants to get home."

"I don't know why you're in such a hurry all of a sudden," says Guthrie pettishly. We take no notice — neither Tony nor I have the slightest desire to renew our acquaintance with the roundabout man.

Guthrie follows us reluctantly, murmuring at intervals that he doesn't know why we are in such a hurry all of a sudden.

The Bentley is now reposing in the car park in solitary state. We pack in, and soon we are buzzing homewards through the darkness, with two bright shafts of light streaming out before us like the beams of a lighthouse. The trees and hedges look a peculiar artificial shade of green in the glare of the lamps, and the white road runs smoothly backwards beneath our wheels.

Tony sets us down at the gate. "Goodbye, Hester," he says, "and thank you for being such a dear. Give my love to old Tim when he rolls up, won't you?"

"But you'll be coming over to see him," I point out. "We'll be here until Tuesday, you know."

"I may — or I may not. It all depends how strong I feel," replies Tony cryptically. "But tell him from me he's a lucky devil."

"Do come on, Hester," says Guthrie impatiently. "I thought you were in such a terrific hurry to get home."

"But now she *is* home, so there's no need to hurry any more," explains Tony kindly.

"I don't know what you're talking about, and what's more you don't know yourself," exclaims Guthrie furiously. "You seem to think I'm half-witted —"

"No, no — not half-witted."

"What do you mean?"

"Think it over when you get into bed," Tony advises him in a soothing voice. "You are bound to understand it in time if you persevere. Just lie flat on your back, and breathe easily through the nose —"

Guthrie turns on his heel with a muttered curse and strides up the drive like a grenadier. I am thankful to see him go without bloodshed.

"What a peppery little fellow he is, to be sure!" exclaims Tony. "Always taking the huff about something, isn't he?"

"It's entirely your fault and you know it," I tell him sternly. "You could wind Guthrie round your finger if

237

you liked — why can't you be nice to him, like you are to me?"

"I'm nice to you, am I?" he enquires in a strange voice.

"Frightfully nice," I reply.

"Well!" he says, "I suppose that's something," and, so saying, he lets in his gear and is gone in a flash.

I follow Guthrie up the drive, and we let ourselves into the quiet house as silently as we can. I can't help smiling to myself, for the darkness and silence of the house remind me of that night when Guthrie and I laid our plans to capture the burglars, and discovered the treasure-seekers instead. Guthrie remembers it too, for I see him glance at the warming pan on the wall with a strange expression on his face.

"What are you thinking of?" I whisper as we creep up the uncarpeted stair.

"Bones," he replies solemnly, and the tone of his voice bodes no good for that lanky individual.

We part at my bedroom door.

"This is the last night, Hester," he says sentimentally. "You won't want me after to-morrow."

I tell him not to be a donkey, and he goes away sorrowfully.

My undressing is soon accomplished, for I am very tired, and I slip into bed and blow out the candle; but for a long time sleep eludes me. To-night is, in a way, the end of my leave. I am longing to see Tim, of course, but I can't help being sorry the fortnight is over. It has been such a complete change from my ordinary life — almost a change of soul. Instead of thinking all the time of my family, and my household affairs, I have been able to think of myself for a whole fortnight — to *be* myself, not just Tim's wife, and the mother of Bryan and Betty. It has been a lovely thing to find that people like me for no other reason than just because they like me.

Is it really only a fortnight since I left Kiltwinkle? It seems years. I have done so much in the time, seen so many beautiful places, and made so many new friends. Mrs. Loudon I knew before, of course, but my feeling for her has grown and deepened; we shall never lose each other now. I love her downright manner and her uncompromising attitude towards life. Guthrie is a new friend well worth having, his simplicity is endearing. (I hope Tim will like Guthrie; somehow I think he will.) I have learnt to know Tony Morley in a different way during these two weeks, to appreciate his real goodness of heart, though I cannot always understand him. Even Mrs. Falconer is nice. Strange as she is I like her, and I know she also likes me. And Deirdre, my Fairy Princess, what of her? Shall we see each other again? I hope so greatly, for she interested me, and I feel that we could be friends if we had the opportunity. I shall always remember, and be glad that I helped her to marry her Fairy Prince.

A score of bright little pictures stand out clearly as I look back over my time at Avielochan. I pick them out and smile over them one by one. My first morning in the garden — the bright, bright sunshine, and the crystal clearness of the air; Guthrie and Elsie fishing on the loch (how hard poor Guthrie struggled to reconcile the rival attractions of love and sport!); the Castle Quill party where I first heard the story of the beautiful Seónaid; the visit to the laundry (I can see the lines of snowy garments dancing in the breeze and hear the soft tones of Miss Campbell's gentle voice); Guthrie's burglars; the picnic when we saw the ghost of Seónaid which turned out to be Deirdre; the dinner-party; Betty's adventure in the mist; my expedition with Tony to Gart-na-Druim with its pleasant memories of our welcome and the beauty of the Western Sea; the elopement of my Fairy Princess; and lastly the fair (a jumble of impressions from which our adventure at the roundabout stands forth as the high light).

Dawn is breaking now, and its pallor creeps in at my open window and spreads like water over the polished floor. Somehow the coming of the new day turns my thoughts to Tim. The page is turned; it is a page of bright colours which will live for ever in my memory. Tim will be here to-morrow — no, *to-day*. At this very moment he is rushing towards me in the train. The same dawn which is creeping in so slowly at my window is breaking over Tim as he rushes through the sleeping land. Dear old Tim — how lovely it will be to have him here! He will enjoy it all so much — the mountains, the forests, the lovely clear air. We shall go fishing together, perhaps we shall climb the hills. We shall laugh together at Mrs. Falconer's rambling stories and Betty's quaint sayings. What was it that Mrs. Loudon said: "Never the time, and the place, and the loved one all together." Lucky me, for I shall have them all!

240

The light brightens and fills the room. A little bird chirps outside my window, and another wakens and answers. Suddenly a perfect choir of little birds bursts into song.

Charlotte Fairlie

D. E. Stevenson

Charlotte Fairlie is a successful, elegant career woman. Still in her 20s, she has landed a job as headmistress of her old school. She is admired and liked by both staff and pupils — but she begins to feel there is something missing in her well-organised life.

Then one summer she goes to stay with a young pupil on the remote Scottish Isle of Targ. In the romantic atmosphere of the Highlands, anything can happen — and even the cool, efficient Charlotte surprises herself . . .

ISBN 0-7531-7614-9 **(hb)**
ISBN 0-7531-7615-7 **(pb)**

The Case of William Smith

Patricia Wentworth

A classic novel from the Golden Age of crime fiction

Miss Wentworth is a first-rate story-teller
Daily Telegraph

Patricia Wentworth has created a great detective in Miss Silver, the little old lady who nobody notices, but who in turn notices everything **Paula Gosling**

For seven years William had worked as a woodcarver for the local toyshop, ignorant of his true identity. The war had robbed him of his memory and no one expected him to find the answer. When William is mysteriously attacked in the street, Miss Silver is called in to help.

Is the attack linked to his forgotten past? Or his recent visit to Eversleys Ltd? As the attacks on William escalate, he and Miss Silver must look into his past to stop the culprits from striking again.

ISBN 0-7531-7584-3 (hb)
ISBN 0-7531-7585-1 (pb)

Bless This House

Norah Lofts

The house was built in the Old Queen's time — built for an Elizabethan pirate who was knighted for the plunder he brought home. It survived many eras, many reigns — it saw the passing of Cromwell and the Civil War. It became rich with an Indian Nabob and poor with a twentieth century innkeeper. It saw wars, and lovers, and death. Children were born there, both heirs and bastards. It had ghosts and legends and a history that grew stranger with every generation.

The house was Merravay — and its story stretched over four hundred years . . .

ISBN 0-7531-7569-X (hb)
ISBN 0-7531-7570-3 (pb)

Artists in Crime

Ngaio Marsh

It started as a student exercise: the knife under the drape, the model's pose chalked in place. But before Agatha Troy, artist and instructor, returns to the class, the pose has been re-enacted in earnest: the model is dead, fixed for ever in one of the most dramatic poses Troy has ever seen.

It's a difficult case for Chief Detective Inspector Alleyn. How can he believe that the woman he loves is a murderess? And yet no one can be above suspicion . . .

ISBN 0-7531-7411-1 (hb)
ISBN 0-7531-7412-X (pb)

Summerhills

D. E. Stevenson

Summerhills continues the story of the lives and loves of the Ayrton family, in particular that of Major Roger Ayrton M.C., his brother and three young half-sisters. Roger has made the Army his career. Anne has settled down as housekeeper to old Mr Orme, the rector. Nell looks after the old house, and it is upon her that the comfort and well-being of the family depend.

A new generation is growing up. The story begins as Roger flies home to Amberwell on leave, full of plans for his family and home.

ISBN 0-7531-7371-9 (hb)
ISBN 0-7531-7372-7 (pb)

ISIS publish a wide range of books in large print, from fiction to biography. Any suggestions for books you would like to see in large print or audio are always welcome. Please send to the Editorial Department at:

ISIS Publishing Limited
7 Centremead
Osney Mead
Oxford OX2 0ES

A full list of titles is available free of charge from:

Ulverscroft Large Print Books Limited

(UK)
The Green
Bradgate Road, Anstey
Leicester LE7 7FU
Tel: (0116) 236 4325

(Australia)
P.O. Box 314
St Leonards
NSW 1590
Tel: (02) 9436 2622

(USA)
P.O. Box 1230
West Seneca
N.Y. 14224-1230
Tel: (716) 674 4270

(Canada)
P.O. Box 80038
Burlington
Ontario L7L 6B1
Tel: (905) 637 8734

(New Zealand)
P.O. Box 456
Feilding
Tel: (06) 323 6828

Details of ISIS complete and unabridged audio books are also available from these offices. Alternatively, contact your local library for details of their collection of ISIS large print and unabridged audio books.